RAIMOND

RAIMOND

THE PATH OF HERO TO MARTYR IS CARVED IN STONE.
THE ROAD FROM SOLDIER TO SAINT IS PAVED BY BLOOD
AND MAGIC.

ANNE MARIE ANDRUS

This is a work of fiction. Any names or characters, businesses or places, events or incidents are fictitious. Any resemblance to persons, living or dead, or actual events is purely coincidental.

Copyright © 2018 Anne Marie Andrus
All rights reserved
ISBN-10: 0-9984155-3-7
ISBN 13: 978-0-9984155-3-6

RAIMOND

THE PATH OF HERO TO MARTYR IS CARVED IN STONE.
THE ROAD FROM SOLDIER TO SAINT IS PAVED BY BLOOD
AND MAGIC.

ANNE MARIE ANDRUS

This is a work of fiction. Any names or characters, businesses or places, events or incidents are fictitious. Any resemblance to persons, living or dead, or actual events is purely coincidental.

Copyright © 2018 Anne Marie Andrus
All rights reserved
ISBN-10: 0-9984155-3-7
ISBN 13: 978-0-9984155-3-6

ALSO BY ANNE MARIE ANDRUS

MONSTERS & ANGELS

The Monsters & Angels Series

THIS BOOK IS DEDICATED TO MY EXTRAORDINARY
READERS,
WHO KNEW RAIMOND WAS THE TRUE STAR OF THIS
SHOW LONG BEFORE I DID.
VIVE LA MAGIE!

PART I
AVELINE

Chapter 1

RISE THE DEMONS
PARIS, FRANCE 1852

IN A DERELICT neighborhood on the fringe of Paris, one burning red eye glowed through the crumbling foundation of a formerly grand hotel. While family and friends still struggled to put the Revolution's gory ugliness behind them, their every move was scrutinized by a trapped predator.

Raimond kept watch, as he had done for decades, until his eye smoldered from distant sunlight. *Switch eyes.* A smile drifted across his face while children scurried behind their parents, shopkeepers threw open their doors and the light of hope shone on every street except one. The worn and rutted surface of Rue Le Cross remained cloaked in darkness.

Footsteps echoed off the cobblestones outside Raimond's portal and he strained to see the trespassers. He flinched at the sight of glowing torches, retreating again into his underground gloom.

A woman barked orders. "Tell those youngsters to stay behind the barricade."

"Go to school, you little fools!" a man called out. "This is no place for kids…or anyone."

"What are you so afraid of husband?"

Raimond stepped forward to hear the man's answer. *I should hope they're scared.*

"I'm not the only one who hears the awful noises in this passage after dark and it's always night on this bloody street."

"Can we just light these lamps and get out of here?" The woman's eyes darted around. "The mayor paid both of us a fortune."

Here they go again. The gas lanterns blazed to life and Raimond drummed his fingers on the wall.

"They're burning," the woman hissed. "But why are they flickering?"

The flames shivered and gasped, as if being blown out by invisible lips. Raimond shook his head.

"This alley is cursed. Every lock is broken. Nothing opens." The man rattled handles and knobs. He froze at the shuttered hotel's rusty door. "Do you hear that?"

Raimond rhythmically smashed a rock on the iron bars of his prison.

"We didn't get paid enough for this wife."

A menacing growl ricocheted off the walls and the couple dropped their torches, slammed into each other and scrambled toward the main street.

Don't come back. Raimond let the rock slip from his grasp and slumped against the dusty wall. *Those doors are jammed shut for a reason.*

As the final, auburn embers of sunlight faded behind the craggy roofline, the underworld groaned to life. Raimond turned around to the absolute black of the catacombs and the squeal of rodents that drowned out hungry cries. He kicked a rat across the cell and his stomach twisted at the whimpers of miserable children sleeping in the cold. They were all victims of a monster that the mortal world above didn't believe existed. He didn't have the heart to tell the little ones they were vampires, too. He sighed. *None of us will ever be warm again.*

Raimond punched walls he'd been beating on for years. A few remaining slivers of stone broke free and he slid to the floor, clawing at his eyes.

Don't fall apart now, soldier. This moment has been years in the making.

As an officer, he'd been expected to sacrifice his life.

Until a maniac stole my soul.

That crime was nothing compared to what the innocents who lived beneath the street with him had endured.

Tonight, it all changes.

In a flash Raimond slammed into iron bars that tore the skin from his forehead. He drew a breath of putrid air.

The villains beat me and I plotted.

He looked at the blackened skin of his hands.

They burned me, and I schemed.

His escape from the torture was a dive into the darkest corners of his mind, and each time he let himself dream, the hallucinations became bloodier and deadlier.

Never mind revenge; I want absolute victory.

His eyes wandered across the dungeon full of unwilling vampires, landing first on a fellow soldier.

Such an odd story, a Scot fighting alongside the French.

Two younger lads slept next to the burly man, both clinging to the ends of a tattered blanket. Nuns, farmers and even patients from the local infirmary had been ripped from their beds and turned into slaves by a madman. In the middle, a young nurse huddled with the frailest children. Her voice, touch and passion to heal had never faltered, despite the hellish conditions.

Convincing these lost souls that they have a future worth living—that will be a challenge.

"How much longer," a boy squeaked through crushing silence, "before that fiend kills us all?"

Heavy chains rattled in a nearby corner, followed by the gruff Scottish accent of Parlan. "Your creator will never kill you, Siras. Just starve you, 'til you're dust."

Siras opened his mouth to reply but stared at the cuffs crushing his ankles instead and said nothing.

"The Commander won't let that happen," a girl quavered. "He promised."

Raimond flexed his hand. The charred skin of his forearm stretched and scraped over tight muscle. Tonight, for the first time, his wrist didn't split open and ooze sludge.

"He hasn't spoken in days," Parlan's neck sagged against a brutally spiked collar. Dried blood stained his chest and arms. "Have you any more matches, wee sister?"

It took the girl four strikes to light the tiny lamp. Her fingers trembled to adjust the flame. "There are no more."

"It's the last one we'll need, *Infirmiere* Aveline."

"Commander? Is that you?" The girl lifted her lamp, throwing slivers of light into the stone and metal cage. "You know my name?"

"*Bien sûr.*" Raimond cleared his throat. "I mean, of course, Nurse Aveline."

"We can speak French, because you know who..." She cringed. "He isn't here."

"Ah, *non*." Raimond held his finger up. "These Scots forced me to learn English over our years together. It's the perfect secret code. Our captors never caught on."

"Are you strong enough though, sir?" Parlan asked. "We've only this one chance."

Raimond nodded. "Tonight's the night."

Aveline raised the lamp as high as she could. "We can survive a little longer."

"You've all suffered dreadfully and I'm to blame." Raimond set his jaw. "This is our *nuit de la liberté.*"

"Independence night," Aveline whispered. "But Commander Raimond, how do we escape?"

The screech of splitting metal was followed by crumbling stone and a resounding crash. When the dust cleared, a man towered in the middle of the prison chamber. Behind his matted beard and grimy skin, red eyes raged with power.

"Your crazy scheme worked." Parlan's eyes burned a dimmer red.

"Indeed, it did." Raimond tore the Scot's chain from the wall, snapped the collar open and pulled him to his feet. "You're free."

Aveline wiped dirty tears from her face. She dug a flask out of her pocket and offered it to Raimond.

"No, my dear. You drink now. You've deferred your rations to me for too long." Raimond placed both hands on her hollow cheeks. "I'll find enough to satisfy everyone."

Aveline sipped blood from the flask and tossed it to Parlan. He took a healthy swig and joined Raimond in freeing the captives.

"Siras, wake up." Parlan shook the redhead's shoulder. "The plan is in motion."

Raimond snapped his fingers. "I'll need my coat back, young man."

"Yes, sir." Siras unfolded the blue fabric he'd been using for a pillow.

Raimond discarded the shredded remnants of his shirt and slipped into his old uniform. He smoothed wrinkles out of the loose coat that used to fit like second skin. With each button he fastened, memories of the last day he wore it flooded his mind. His long fingers paused at a jagged hole in the left chest pocket.

"That one bullet," Parlan muttered. "Always seemed like—"

"An assassination?" Raimond turned to a crowd of bedraggled vampires filling the chamber. "I still believe the Allemands were responsible. Their motivation, though, remains a mystery."

"I'm so hungry, my bones feel like splinters." Siras stifled a moan and gestured to the pale faces behind him. "We're all starving, sir."

"Parlan and I will remedy that." Raimond squared his shoulders. "You and Anton…Anton, where are you?"

A skinny boy held up his hand and hopped forward. "Here, sir."

"Excellent. You'll guard the door while we hunt."

"But what if…" Siras shuffled his feet and nudged Anton's arm. "You know, *he* comes back?"

Raimond stood rigid. "Faison."

A collective gasp rose from the basement.

"Starting tonight," Raimond pointed around the room, "we say his name."

"But, we never." Aveline tugged his sleeve.

"It's the first step in destroying his power." Raimond patted Aveline's shoulder and made eye contact with everyone in the little crowd. "Faison is psychotic, but after all these years, highly predictable. He was here two nights ago and won't return for five more."

Anton leaned in. "Covered in leather—"

"Head to toe," Siras whispered. "Such a—"

"Ghoul." Anton nodded.

"Gentlemen!" Parlan clapped once. "The Commander is speaking."

"They are correct. Faison is the ultimate ghoul." Raimond clasped his hands behind his back. "So, in five nights, we need to be—we *will* be—fierce and ready."

Chapter 2
PECULIAR BEATS

RAIMOND YANKED THE door open and ducked onto colorless Rue Le Cross with Parlan staggering behind him. He grabbed the Scot's arm and felt ground glass shift under loose skin as if his muscles had disintegrated. "You need to drink, friend."

"Never mind me. There are ladies and wee ones suffering in that basement." Parlan's voice jumped. "What kind of depraved creature causes pain like that?"

"At this point, even the soldiers we trained don't remember anything but killing and following that madman's orders." Raimond crept to the edge of the main street and looked both ways into the blue murk. "Our premiere job now is to teach them a new way to feed, so they can survive and stay hidden."

"We must learn first."

"I've been working on it." Raimond rubbed his forehead. "With varying degrees of failure."

"Yes, well, the consequences of not supplying your quota of blood to Faison were escalating." Parlan scowled at the scorched skin on Raimond's arms. "Aveline is a gifted healer and nothing she did helped. Not even a bit."

"We're different beings now. The old ways are no longer effective."

"You mean the human ways?"

Raimond nodded and held a finger to his lips. "We need fresh eyes and new methods. I'll make that happen."

"I pray you're right." Parlan flattened his back against a crumbling wall. "What about him?"

Raimond followed Parlan's gaze to a hulk of a man.

The drunk stumbled along the curb, singing and waving the bottle in his hand like the official banner of intoxication.

"Looks like a good one to learn on. Certainly not a dainty flower." Raimond chuckled and nudged Parlan's shoulder. "Let's get on with it."

Both vampires fell into step with the jolly drunk and steered him into the shadows of an abandoned warehouse

"We're goin' the wrong way." The man smacked himself in the face twice, attempting to hold his nose. "You two blokes need a bath."

"Fair point." Raimond stepped in front of the man and captured his stare.

Parlan watched intently as Raimond convinced their victim to settle on an old crate as if it was a velvet chair in front of a crackling fire. In the past, he would have merely knocked the man unconscious and dragged him underground.

Parlan scratched his head. "Almost like you're forcing your will into his skull."

"Exactly like that, but he needs to relax a bit more." Raimond slapped the drunk's shoulder. "*Monsieur*, what's the difference between a light in a cave and a dance in an inn? One is a taper in a cavern and the other is a caper in a tavern."

The drunk drew invisible calculations in the air before breaking out into laughter.

"Look at that, Parlan!" Raimond held his arms out. "He's got it."

Parlan gave a weak thumbs up. "You, on the other hand, may be losing it."

"This one's even better. Why are two young ladies kissing each other an emblem of Christianity?" Raimond turned to his companion. "Soldier?"

"They are doing unto each other, as they would have men do unto them." Parlan couldn't hide his smile.

Neither vampire tried to disguise their darkening skin or the fangs that pierced their gums.

Raimond locked his gaze onto the drunk's eyes again.

"Never mind the bath, mister." The man rolled his sleeve up far enough to expose the tender flesh inside of his elbow. "You and your pal need to visit a dentist."

Parlan's smile faded as he shuffled back a few steps. "Should be easy enough to maintain self-control."

"Even you don't believe that." Raimond fought the fire that shot from his throat to his belly and back again. He sunk his fangs into the man's pasty arm, listened to the rhythmic pulsing of arteries and steeled himself before piercing the barrier. Two gulps of blood cooled the burning, another took the ragged edge off his thirst.

"Why did you stop?" Parlan stared at Raimond kneeling on the floor, cradling the man's bleeding limb. "You're shaking."

Raimond took a deep breath, stood and nicked his own wrist. Tiny drops of his blood healed the drunk's wounds without a trace. "Your turn. Avoid the neck, for now."

"That was not nearly enough to satiate you." Parlan edged closer to the human and forced a smile. He looked at Raimond in astonishment when the man grinned back. "I can honestly say my prey have never been so jolly."

Parlan needed Raimond's help to stop drinking before he damaged the man beyond repair.

"How in the world do you know when to end it?" Parlan clamped his fist onto window bars in the alley and dragged himself away.

"His heartbeat became eccentric." Raimond healed their victim again and propped him up on the crate, with a bottle in his hand. "If you can't hear it, feel it in your eardrums."

Parlan massaged his own neck, cracked his jaw and moved onto adjusting each finger.

"Must you do that?" Raimond asked. "It's revolting."

9

The Scot plucked the bottle from the drunk's fingers, took a swig and replaced it. "All this ghoulery, and cracking my knuckles revolts you?"

"Makes my spine crawl." Raimond stood at his full height and softened his tone. "So, aside from your rickety joints…"

"I feel quite a bit stronger but you move much faster. Almost a blur."

"Drink more, you'll move like a flash too." Raimond smirked. "The color in your face seems a brighter white. Hair is still grey."

"As it will always be. We could teach your new method to our comrades."

"Not on him, though." Raimond snapped his fingers. The drunk's eyes slid shut and he descended into peaceful sleep. "He must have inebriated friends."

"We'll need to show the others, one at a time, so they don't tear people apart." Parlan peered down the street. "They're ravenous."

"It's almost closing time for the pubs," Raimond said. "We'll feed the troops, then follow this guy's advice and take a bath."

"Odd priorities for a monster."

"Think about it." Raimond rubbed his palms together. "If we blend into civilized society, we can drink more powerful blood. That's how we beat Faison."

"The thought control." Parlan drooled as he stepped in front of two stumbling figures in the street. "I should know how to do it, but…"

"It takes practice." Raimond's move behind the men, an enhanced flash, cut off their escape route. "I will assist with genuine pleasure, but there is one more wrinkle."

Parlan made quick work of the humans, drinking from the bulging arteries in their necks, pulling away before Raimond had to intervene, leaving their shirt collars as pristine and blood-free as before the attack. "What more could I ask for?"

"Absorbing." Raimond held his palms out.

"You have gone mad." Parlan dropped his voice. "Is that part of the survival technique?"

"Another ingredient of my grand plan." Raimond sighed and pointed to the last man's eyes. "Sit back and focus. Read his consciousness and tell me what you see."

Parlan grunted and followed the instructions. "White jacket, mortar and pestle, customers…a pharmacy?"

"Correct." Raimond nodded and rolled his hand in a circle. "Keep going."

"He helps people. Follows doctor's orders for potions and poultices." Parlan rubbed his beard. "He's a local hero?"

"And the community loves him," Raimond said. "You can't be him, but you can take the essence of his being."

"The good things…but does he feel me do it? Do I hurt him?"

"Aside from a mild headache," Raimond steered the man to a bench in a tiny park, "I don't think he'll notice a thing."

"This is what we can sell to our family members who have been suffering for years. This could give them their lives back. Almost."

Men's shouts burst into the desolate street as the pub door slammed open. Patrons stumbled into the dingy snow, shook hands and lurched in varied directions searching for their own front doors. The vampires intercepted three men the moment they stepped away from the safety of the streetlamps.

"*Excusez moi.*" Raimond tapped the straggler on the shoulder and flashed a wide smile. "Could you and your friends spare a moment to help my children?"

After convincing one of the group to donate matches and candles from his shop and another to gather scarves and mittens knit for tiny hands, Raimond kept his promise and delivered fresh blood to his starving friends. He and Parlan stood by to minimize the damage and preserve the lives of their donors. Further instructions on feeding without killing would have to wait for another night.

"What are you going to do with all that?" Parlan pointed to the decorated foil bags left by a candy shop owner. Raimond shrugged and shoved them in his pocket. "I'm sure we'll find a use for it."

By the time the sun rose over Paris, the pub customers were safely home in their beds. Scores of candles banished despair from the catacomb under Rue Le Cross. Raimond kept watch while all his companions fell into a well-fed slumber. The youngest ones snuggled into clean clothing made from festive wool. The soldiers wrapped fresh blankets around their shoulders. A few actually snored.

Parlan carried the biggest candle to the table in the center of the chamber and joined his commander. He warmed his palms over the triple wicks. "It's like a little bonfire."

A tin cup of blood sat between them. Raimond sniffed around the rim before taking a sip. "Starting to sour."

"It's only been an hour since you tapped that bloke's vein. There must be a way to preserve it and build a portable stockpile."

"Worst part is, we've been living like this for over twenty years—"

"Lord have mercy." Parlan clenched his fists. "The time, the waste."

"My fault. A pitiful lack of courage. Faison's beatings, I could survive, but the threats to them and you—"

"Starvation and terror. His manipulation was sadistic and genius at the same time."

Raimond's eyes darted around the room and landed on children sleeping in each other's arms. "Waiting for the stars to align was—"

"Essential. Imperative." Parlan raised his chin and saluted. "Flawless instinct."

"You realize we know nothing?" Raimond leaned forward in his rickety chair. "Like newborns."

"Along with most Highland folk, I've always believed our kind existed...as a fairy tale." Parlan rested his elbows on the table. "Apparently, I was wrong. Oh, and gold daggers are lethal."

"Gold? I assumed silver. We have neither." Raimond blew out a long breath. "How do we learn the rest? Who's our teacher?"

"Me."

Both men whirled around and squinted into the flickering haze.

"Aveline?" Raimond waved her over. "What can you tell us, *mademoiselle?*"

"Faison never knew this." Aveline pointed to Parlan. "I saw him get turned. I remember every awful detail."

Raimond patted the stool next to his. "*S'il vous plaît.*"

"After Parlan was speared, Faison's soldiers found him and summoned their master." Aveline flopped into the chair. "What he did to him was barbaric."

The young nurse wrung her hands and told her story in snippets. She faltered, began to weep, but both men urged her to continue.

Raimond offered her the rest of the blood in the tin cup. "So, Faison drained Parlan's blood and, repeat that next portion…about his chest."

Aveline held up her fist. "That horrible man drove through flesh and bone and everything in the way, like it was paper. He held Parlan's heart in his hand and mimicked a heartbeat. Slow and steady at first, growing in intensity, spreading his depraved venom."

Parlan swallowed hard. "And then?"

"He must have felt a stir. Your body dropped to the pavement like a sack of rubbish." Aveline brushed pink tears from her cheeks. "Seven drops of blood completed your transformation."

"From whom?" Parlan leaned forward. "These secrets will help all of us, I promise."

Aveline pointed to a cherub with brown skin, clutching a rag doll in her peaceful sleep. "She was still human, but not for long."

Parlan's eyes bulged as he shook his head.

"Not much younger than you when it happened?" Raimond patted Aveline's hand.

"How young do you think I am?" Aveline tucked a lock of raven hair behind her ear. "Or was?"

Parlan shrugged weakly. "Twelve?"

"Oh, my." Aveline dropped her head in her hands and laughed. "I was eighteen. Proper and marriageable, though I'd been ill for a few months and lost a bit of weight."

Parlan and Raimond stared at each other and then back at her.

"I had recurring pain." Aveline rubbed her belly. "First, I thought I was with child. Please, don't think less of me. At the time, an old-fashioned engagement seemed…"

"Like a fancy dream?" Raimond asked.

"And, a waste of time none of us had. The doctors performed some minor procedures, looking for abscess. They could find no infection and certainly, no child." Aveline wrapped the blanket tighter around her back. "They assured me that surgery would be painless. I agreed, but…"

"Faison's attack happened first?" Parlan asked.

"Well," Aveline's shoulders slumped. "More like during the operation. Before they finished stitching me up."

"That is a true nightmare." Raimond groaned. "Do you still have the pain, dear?"

"Comes and goes. More when I drink too quickly." Aveline's gaze drifted toward the darkness. "I hear whimpering. Poor little ones."

"I can assist." Parlan stood and helped Aveline to her feet.

"Thank you." Aveline dropped her wrap on the back of the old chair. "Thank you both."

"No, *merci mademoiselle*." Raimond nodded as she walked away. He began folding her blanket and froze. The fabric fell open revealing a fresh black bloodstain. Raimond's eyes darted to the shadowy figure of Aveline. Her olive skin glowed bronze in the warm candlelight while she cradled two toddlers in her arms as if nothing were wrong.

Chapter 3

SECRETS & ERRORS

GOLDEN POOLS OF light spilled from gas lanterns, inviting the well-heeled citizens to linger in the nighttime streets of Paris.

"At least we know more, now." Raimond clapped Parlan on the shoulder. "Hard facts, disturbing as they are."

"The process for creating one of…us." Parlan balled his fists. "How could we not know for all these years?"

"Because knowledge is power, and Faison wanted us firmly under his thumb."

"He controlled us so well, we never even wondered." Parlan forced his fingers to relax. "I don't want to think about that, or him, anymore. How soon can we teach the little ones to tap energy the way you showed me?"

"I need to perfect my methods. There may be pitfalls." Raimond held the pub door open for Parlan. Inside, a freshly varnished bar gleamed in front of a wall of exotic liquors.

"You look quite distinguished with your new haircut."

"Let's hope it doesn't grow back like a magic trick and cause a stir." He threaded his way through the crowd, discreetly sniffing each patron until he settled on a specific man. "*Bonsoir, monsieur.* May I buy you a drink?"

The man nodded at Raimond's silver coin, moved his black bag to the floor and signaled the barkeep. "Another brandy for me, and for this fine gentleman?"

"I'll have the same."

"Are you a visitor to Paris?"

"No, I've lived here for years in the Saint Germain." Raimond eased onto the empty stool and gently pried into the man's conscience with his mind. "You're the local physician?"

"*Oui*, and a professor at the university. We're making great strides in research." He sipped his brandy from an elegant snifter, looked Raimond up and down and shrugged. "In twenty years, we'll be able to perform surgery that will extend human life for decades, I believe."

"Longer life? I do think that's a reason to celebrate."

"As long as everyone is happy and healthy." The doctor's smile drooped into a grim twist. "Saving lives, here and now, is just as essential."

"You run a free clinic...I've heard of your generosity." The man rubbed his forehead and Raimond frowned. "Are you unwell?"

"No, merely another late night. That's the life of a doctor. Always in a crowd...forever alone."

"If I had my life to do over, I'd be like you." Raimond lifted his glass and set it back down, without drinking. "A healer and a savior. Someone to be proud of."

"You look young enough to follow your dreams, wherever they lead you." The doctor finished the last of his brandy. "Just remember, you're only as good as your support system. Treat your colleagues, especially the nurses, like treasure—you'll reap the rewards."

"But how, *Docteur*?"

"You're in Paris." The man pointed out a foggy window. "The sky is the only limit."

"And beyond France?"

"Doctors from London and Edinburgh have established legitimate medical schools in the colonies."

"You mean America?"

"I'm an old man." The doctor winked. "Medical progress is exhilarating, but I leave the world of politics to others. If you do cross the Atlantic, I recommend universities in Philadelphia or Boston. If you don't fancy city shenanigans, Georgia's newly established college is accepting students. Best of luck to you."

The doctor slipped on his coat and meandered to the door.

Parlan glided onto the vacated bar stool. "That seemed like more than an ideological meal."

Raimond rubbed the center of his chest. "I want to be that man."

"A mortal teacher and servant of the sick. Isn't that a step down from Commander?"

"No, it's perfect. My father was vehemently against me joining the resistance. He was determined that I was to be a doctor."

Raimond and Parlan strolled home from the pub, darting under awnings and balconies to dodge raindrops. Anton and Siras flashed around a corner with more supernatural speed than they could control, shattering the peaceful evening. The twins collided and wound up sprawled on the damp cobblestones.

"We meant well." Anton clawed onto Parlan's coat and dragged himself upright. "I swear it!"

"What the devil has gotten into you two?" Parlan redirected Siras' arm before he yanked on Raimond's jacket.

Siras covered his eyes. "We need your help to fix a mistake—"

"Our mistake." Anton pressed his palms together. "But with the best intentions. I promise."

Raimond looked down the dark street. "What is that racket?"

"We tried to save him." Siras pointed behind him. "But he won't stop—"

"Screaming." Anton clamped his hands over his ears. "Something's wrong."

Aveline swept out of the fog like a ghost in her dove-grey nursing cape. She plunked her hands on her hips. "We have a severe problem."

"Who's howling like a wounded dog?" Raimond charged down the street. Anton and Siras followed.

Anton waved his right hand in the air. "The man with no—"

"He lost his arm." Siras stumbled as he turned to Parlan. "You know who I mean."

"The beggar?" Parlan grabbed Siras' shirt. "What the hell did you do to him?"

All four men stopped short in front of a disheveled figure. Between shrieks, he muttered unintelligible words.

"He was always so kind to us." Anton shrunk back. "We just thought—"

"If we could make him whole." Siras' knees buckled. "We would be good men again."

"You gave him your blood?" Raimond asked.

Anton and Siras nodded furiously.

"This was an old injury." Aveline unspooled soaked bandages. "There are things even our blood can't heal."

"He looks possessed." Parlan grabbed for the man's thrashing hands. "Is it pain?"

"If it was simple pain, I could fix it." Aveline pulled a potion bottle from her skirt and poured it down the man's throat. "Part of the human mind shields the body from shock. That's being ripped apart, along with every bit of healed tissue."

The man focused one of his wobbling eyes on Raimond. "Help me, I'll never survive this torture again."

Raimond and Aveline shared a frown. She shook her head and pointed at the bloody stump that grew more ragged by the minute.

"You can set me free." The man crawled to Raimond's feet. "I'm begging you."

Raimond sunk to his knees. "Sir, do you realize what you're asking of me?"

"I do, and I know what you are."

The circle of vampires traded uneasy stares.

"Bless you boys for trying to save me." The man's shaky finger pointed to Anton and Siras. "You came to France to fight—to defend helpless people and you still carry that light within you. I wasn't always this way, a homeless wretch."

"Of course not," Raimond took the man's crooked hand. "Tell me your story."

"My family was starving in this filthy city. I had a little son...got caught stealing a spoiled apple from a street vendor."

Aveline rubbed the man's shoulder. "And you confessed to the crime?"

"So those vicious police took my hand instead of his. Over a piece of rotten fruit—" He gasped and spit blood. "Made my wife promise to run and never look back."

Raimond fixed his gaze on the old man's eyes and searched his mind. "She was your childhood sweetheart."

"Loved her more than—" He gritted his teeth and wheezed. "Anything in this world."

"Your story is safe with me, for eternity." Raimond lowered his forehead to the man's hand, absorbed every memory and then stepped away while Aveline comforted him.

Parlan passed Raimond a steel blade. "He's human, this should be plenty."

Anton and Siras gaped at the weapon and cringed.

Aveline pulled a handkerchief from her cape pocket, drizzled oil onto the lace and held it in front of the man's face. "Breathe deep, kind soul."

"Smells sweet and endless, like jasmine on a hot summer night. I'm ready to meet the Almighty."

Raimond waited until the beggar drifted into a stupor and sliced his throat with precision, from ear to ear. Bright red blood was followed by a flood of black clots and liquid slime.

"It's a miracle he survived long enough to talk." Aveline lowered his body to the cobblestones.

Before his dying heart beat five times, the man's spirit burst into the night sky. The misty figure smiled at them before waving goodbye with both hands and shooting toward heaven.

Aveline lifted the blade from Raimond's hand with her fingertips and ran her handkerchief along the steel. "All clean." She looked at Raimond's face and froze. "Your eyes are green."

Raimond shrugged. "Back when I was born, maybe."

Parlan flashed behind Aveline and stared. "They're green now."

"Like mint." Aveline inched closer. "But that's not—don't you see silhouettes of tiny houses and crosses?"

"Do I see what?" Parlan squinted. "No."

Raimond's chuckle was cut short by Aveline's frown. "You're scaring me."

"The vision slipped away, but...it would be so rare." Aveline shook her head and handed him a leather cord. "You need another barber's visit."

"Already?" Raimond swept the hair off his shoulders and wrapped it in the tie. "Miserable rain, spoiled my new style in one night."

"I'll see you men at home." Aveline touched Raimond's cheek. "After I check my grimoire."

Raimond watched the grey cape's sapphire lining swirl around the corner. He turned to Parlan. "Her what?"

Chapter 4

To The Wild Country

LATE THE FOLLOWING night, Raimond paced the floor of a shuttered bar on the corner of Rue Le Cross. He checked that the door was locked and adjusted the faded closed sign. Turning, he clenched his fists, grunted and kicked over a row of rickety chairs. "Damn! Bloody!" He raised his foot to send another stool flying but caught himself. "Hell."

Parlan nodded and chewed the inside of his cheek. "Uh, scotch?"

Raimond righted a chair and slouched down at Parlan's crooked table. "I...apologize for the outburst."

"Faison will be here soon enough."

"I feel unprepared...like I'm missing something important."

Parlan slid the bottle over, followed by a chipped tumbler. "But that's not the only thing troubling you."

Raimond splashed pale liquor in the glass, drained it in one swallow and gagged. "Is that the best bottle in this entire stock?"

"You're the one who chose this dismal establishment. Tell me what really has you in such turmoil."

"We've built a friendship during our captivity, *oui?*"

"I wagered my life on it, Commander."

"Served together, before that. Swore the same oath. You were the most loyal man in my battalion."

"But?" Parlan poured a drink and glowered at it.

Raimond fished a coin from his pocket and spun it on the tabletop. The copper piece skidded over a crack in the veneer and fell flat. He began to spin it again and seized it in his hand instead. "We've planned missions, mapped out attacks, kept each other awake on night watch."

"You may be the only commander in history to take wretched night watch with his soldiers."

"I never expected my men to do anything I didn't do myself."

"Ask your question." Parlan pushed the scotch across the table. "Or drink this."

"Anything but that." Raimond shoved the bottle back. "I think the chances are very good that you and I have been reborn as brothers."

"If that's true and we are family, our curse could be a blessing of sorts."

"A large family harbors incredible strength."

Parlan raised an eyebrow and grinned. "When they get along."

"It's something I didn't have growing up." Raimond drummed his fingers on the table. "As a young man, I dreamed of a houseful of sons and daughters."

"What other dreams do you have?"

Raimond closed his eyes and exhaled. "Freedom."

"Which I have every confidence we shall win." Parlan brandished the Scotch. "What else?"

"That you don't drink this swill." Raimond intercepted the bottle. "And to be a doctor."

"Still?" Parlan's sly smile grew to a wide grin. "My brother, the esteemed Dr. Banitierre."

Raimond cleared his throat. "Let's not get ahead of ourselves. I wonder, is there proof anywhere that we actually are brothers?"

A muffled knock at the back door made Raimond leap from his chair. He peeked through the keyhole and relaxed before letting Aveline in and resetting the old tumblers. He and Parlan exchanged glances and pointed to her at the same time.

"You're exactly the voice of reason we need right now." Parlan caught Aveline's arm as she stumbled. He pulled out a seat. "What's wrong?"

"Not a thing." Aveline righted herself on the old chair and produced a bottle of wine. "What was that about needing a voice?"

"She brought decent wine." Raimond raised the bottle to his mouth, gripped the cork in his teeth and popped it free. He looked for any obvious signs of bleeding as Aveline sat down. "Almost feel guilty asking for anything else, but I'm curious…your odd comment about my eyes."

"I'm researching that, I promise." Aveline's fingers trembled. "I know you have bigger questions."

Parlan slid his stool closer. He picked up her hand and shot Raimond a sharp look. "Have you been feeding enough, dear?"

"As much as I can. The rest of our little clan need it more," Aveline said. "Ask me your questions, before you get drunk."

"Well, we know you saw Faison turn Parlan." Raimond set the wine on the table. "But what about me?"

"Whatever happened to you, Commander, was a highly guarded secret. But I know Faison wanted absolute control. We can make an educated guess." Aveline took a swallow of wine. "The only way to truly prove bloodline is from the book."

"Book?" Parlan asked.

Raimond dropped his head and sighed.

"You soldiers really don't know?" Aveline rested her elbows on the table and kept it from tipping over with her shoe. "Every family has a sacred book, chronologically listing the original sire and all offspring."

"We're blessed to have you." Raimond touched her arm. "I see you're wearing your nursing uniform again."

"I think I missed it more than I realized. My family have been healers for centuries. Back in the dark days…or should I say, darker days…when medicine was a black art."

Raimond ran his fingers across sapphire initials embroidered on her sleeve. "What does the R stand for?"

"Roussel, but keep that a secret." Aveline tucked her hand under her cape and shivered. "All my surviving kin have fled France to…who knows where."

Parlan slipped his coat off and wrapped it around her shoulders. "You shouldn't be able to feel the cold."

"But the memory of it chills me to the bone." Aveline pushed the wine away. "It may be difficult to find Faison's book, but it must exist. Your names are already written, in blood ink, on your very own pages."

"Brothers." Parlan grabbed Raimond's arm. "A formidable team."

"Most likely, but…" Raimond rolled off his chair. "I'm a single child, the only remaining Banitierre."

Parlan's palm shot into the air. "I have extensive family back in the high country."

"And they would welcome…" Raimond swept his hand out. "Our kind?"

"With open arms." Parlan nodded. "I have no doubt."

"We'll come back to this subject in a moment." Raimond stood at the end of the table. "During our captivity, was I the only one who noticed the blue-eyed vampires?"

"The vicious ones?" Parlan nodded. "Oh, I saw them too."

"My guess is they're Rakshasa." Aveline pinged back and forth between the men's blank stares. "An ancient species from the Himalayan mountains, at least that's the legend. Faison seemed afraid of them as well."

"They never turned anyone." Raimond paced. "But—"

"They abducted enough poor souls." Aveline twisted her fingers. "I'll try to learn more."

"Cautiously, please. Back to happier topics…Parlan, I know you weren't related to Anton and Siras by Scottish blood," Raimond tapped his chin. "Yet, they too are our brothers."

"In fact, they've claimed to be twins." Parlan shook his head. "I only see a resemblance in their eyes."

"They're both short. Other than that, they couldn't be more different." Raimond chuckled. "Except they complete each other's sentences."

"Another inseparable pair," Parlan said. "They insisted on giving that lonely beggar a proper burial, in a real cemetery."

Raimond pinched the bridge of his nose. "I think we all learned a lesson from that unfortunate incident, about what our blood can and cannot do."

Parlan nodded. "Old injuries are permanent."

"Never underestimate the complexities of the mind." Aveline tucked Parlan's coat tighter around her chest. "What you did for him, though, taking his memories so he could die in peace…that was powerful. Almost divine."

Parlan glanced around and chuckled. "Were angels singing?"

"You'd be surprised how many guardians walk amongst us, singing off key." Aveline patted Parlan's arm. "Honestly, I'm not sure why the moment struck me so hard, but I'll figure it out." She slumped back and drew wrapped packages from her pocket.

"What's that?" Parlan pointed to the parcels.

"Gifts." Aveline placed them on the table. "I'll explain as soon as I catch my breath."

"Before we engage Faison, we need to agree on an escape plan." Raimond stepped behind Aveline's chair and held the back of his hand to her forehead, checking for fever.

"Absolutely…" Parlan blinked hard. "Not leaving you."

"He's right." Aveline gently brushed Raimond away. "What if something awful happens and we need to split up? I'm sure you've noticed that the rest of our little family hasn't gained strength the way you hoped. They've fed well, but most were so weak when they were turned…they need to be protected."

Parlan and Raimond stared at each other. Night air in the abandoned bar hung like a ragged velvet curtain around them.

"We've come so far—" Raimond pounded his fist on the table. "The escape plan will be for the safety of all."

Parlan sighed. "We'll address it this one time, and never again."

"I'm finished with Paris." Raimond opened his mouth to continue but paced the room instead. His fingers trailed along the old bar top, sinking into gouges and scars where the polish had been worn away by countless hands. "My parents..."

"You rarely speak of them, brother."

"Because they've vanished. Two devout, honest, and hardworking people who earned a better fate." Raimond slumped against a peeling wall. "Once I got my bearings, I searched everywhere. Faison will pay dearly."

"Raimond, for you." Aveline held out the brown bundles. "And one for you, Parlan."

Raimond untied a delicate ribbon and unwrapped a pocket-sized diary. He ran his fingers over the red binding and carved leather shapes on the cover. "Angel's wings?"

Parlan held his own diary up to the candle light. "Mine's a twelve-point stag."

"I know you both worry about forgetting details." Aveline reached over and opened Raimond's journal. "You can write anything on those silver-lined pages. But only you will be able to read it. Well, you and me. Try it."

Raimond found a pen behind the bar, scrolled a few words and showed it to Parlan. "Anything?"

"Blank." Parlan printed a few lines in his book and studied Aveline's face. "You're full of surprises."

"Only a few. Back to Faison, whose evil knows no bounds," Aveline said. "I always believed his killings were random. Perhaps not in Raimond's case."

"Seems like a well-orchestrated plot and we'll get to the bottom of it." Parlan started to pour wine into his glass. He opted to gulp from the bottle instead. "If I ever need to disappear in an emergency, I'll make a run for Scotland."

"And I for the coast, where I can secure passage to...anywhere but here." Raimond set his jaw. "I'll find you, brother."

"What if we don't get separated?" Aveline asked. "I mean, Scotland sounds like an enchanting destination to me."

"I've been hearing about it forever," Raimond said. "I'd love to see it with my own eyes."

"What I've dreamed of, all these years," Parlan slumped back in his chair and pressed his palms together, "is going home."

"If any angels are listening," Raimond squeezed Aveline's outstretched hand, "may we all find a safe home again."

"Tell me what you wrote in the book, brother. The curiosity may kill me."

"Tell me yours, first." Raimond sat back and smirked.

Parlan flipped to the blank front page and showed it to Aveline.

"Perfect." Aveline nodded.

Parlan traced the invisible letters for Raimond. "Brothers of the Renegade Blood."

Raimond tapped his white page. "So, it begins."

"So, it does. Once we've had our revenge, we'll set a course for the hills north of Inverness where my Lutaire name is legendary. To family!" Parlan emptied the remaining wine into three glasses and offered a toast. "To the wild country!"

Chapter 5

BECAUSE SHE ASKED

DUSK OF THE sixth night exploded into chaos.

"Someone's coming!" Siras barreled through the basement door. "Many strangers."

Anton rushed in behind him with wide eyes. "Too many."

"Get in position!" Raimond leapt up and shoved everyone into their corners. He darted toward his crumbled cage and wrinkled his brow, ducking into shadows next to the stairs instead. "No time."

Parlan heaved himself backward against the opposite wall. "We'll improvise."

"Humans." Raimond held up one shaky finger. The first figures slumped through the door and he exhaled. "Terrified ones with weak blood. Not meant for drinking."

"I see the scorpion crest." Parlan craned his neck farther around the stones. "One soldier. No Faison."

"More slaves?" Aveline poked her head around the corner. "How many does the ogre need?"

"Aveline!" Siras and Anton yanked her back.

Once the door swung shut, Parlan jumped on the solitary guard.

"Should we kill him?" Raimond joined the scuffle, holding the guard's neck in the crook of his elbow.

"I recognize that cruel bastard." Aveline shook her fists. "Cut off his despicable head."

Parlan punched the guard in the face and stole his sword.

"You know what would be better?" Aveline hissed. "Rip his heart out."

"If you really want me to—" Raimond hunched over and dragged his palms up his pant legs. The green irises of his eyes erupted into red flames seconds before he plunged his fangs into the guard's back. Flesh stretched before breaking apart with the wail of shattering metal. Drenched in black blood, he pulled back before focusing his attack on the man's spine.

"Raimond!" Aveline swept children into her skirts and clamped her hands over their eyes. "I didn't mean—"

Almost all the prisoners gagged at the sound of splintering bone and the pop of vessels tearing free, one at a time. The rest searched for an escape, crashing into stone walls as the dying guard vomited foul slop.

Siras nudged Anton's arm. "I've never seen him so—"

"Fierce." Anton squared his shoulders. "Like a hero."

Raimond shook the heart in his fangs and seized it with both hands, grinding the tissue into scraps with his fingers.

A young girl in a pink shawl watched with eyes like saucers. Her jaw dropped and the color drained from her face.

"For heaven's sake." Aveline dove to the floor and caught the girl as she fainted. "Removing it with your hand would have been enough."

"I'm sorry, so sorry." Raimond dropped the heart fragments. He sunk to his knees in front of the frightened crowd. "Everyone's safe, I promise." His blank eyes darted to Aveline.

"No, I'm sorry. You did that because I told you to." Aveline tossed him a wet cloth. "They won't remember a thing. We'll make sure of it."

Parlan pointed to Anton and Siras. "Lads, find some food, you know...people food."

Siras plucked the sword from the dead guard's belt. "Could be useful."

"This too." Anton found a gold dagger in the man's pocket. "Things are looking up."

"These folks need a meal, make it quick." Raimond shoved them out the door. He scrubbed his face clean. "What the hell came over me?"

"Years of cruelty and abuse," Parlan took the bloody cloth, "does things to a man."

"Unacceptable." Raimond peeled off his stained shirt. "That will not be my...our legacy."

"Everyone will eat in a few minutes." Aveline urged the disheveled bunch into a back room. She handed out blankets while Parlan poured tea in dented metal cups. "Then Raimond will tell you a story, one at a time."

"If you listen to me, this will all go away, as if it never happened." Raimond motioned for everyone to gather around. "Who wants to talk first?"

"Me." The girl in the pink shawl stepped forward.

Raimond placed his hand under her chin. "What's your name?"

"I...I forget."

"Your memory will come back." Raimond crouched down. "Where do you live?"

"By the brook? Does that help?"

"Yes, it does." Raimond tucked a strand of hair behind her ear. "How about we call you Brook?"

"I like that." Brook smiled. "Are you a doctor?"

Raimond shook his head and looked at Aveline, mixing herbs for a poultice and holding an elderly woman's hand at the same time. "Maybe someday. The nurse is the boss here."

One by one, he erased dreadful memories from every victim and considered their smiles as his reward. With the rescued prisoners safely upstairs in the main rooms of the old inn, Raimond walked through one more time, pouring extra tea in cups and tucking wraps around children.

"Thank you, sir." Brook grabbed his pant leg as he passed.

"You're a very brave girl, you know?"

Brook pointed across the dirty basement to Aveline. "What about her? She's pretty."

"*Oui.*" Raimond dug in his pocket and handed the little girl a glittery foil-wrapped candy. "Yes, she is."

Chapter 6

CURTAIN CALL

ON THE SEVENTH night, Faison and his thugs stalked through the dark streets of Paris. Aveline held her ear to the dirty floor and updated their progress, block by block. At midnight, the villains invaded the dank catacombs of Rue Le Cross. This time, Raimond and his followers were poised and waiting. In the front rooms, the littlest vampires feigned sleep, tangled in old sheets and filthy clothes as they had done for years. Once Faison and his three bodyguards passed through the door to the most secure chamber, it was slammed and barred from the outside. Raimond and Parlan attacked from the murky corners. Like synchronized murderers, each vampire took three steps and slit a guard's throat before their boss turned around.

Parlan ripped their capes off and tossed black silk onto smoldering candles. Flames erupted and lit the entire chamber as if it were high noon.

Faison stumbled into the ruin of Raimond's old cage and was met with Aveline's gold blade, aimed at his heart. The maniacal laugh that bubbled from his chest choked to a snort at her wild lunge. He jumped back, narrowly avoiding the dagger's point. Whirling around, he addressed the men. "I knew changing the vapid nurse was a mistake…most likely the Scot too, but not Commander Banitierre."

Raimond balled his fists. Dark veins exploded across his face and down his neck like roots searching for water.

Faison twitched his gloved fingers. "He is the magnificent monster I always knew he would be."

Parlan sprung forward. "Should I be offended?"

"If you've energy to waste, wild man. All of you here were feeble prey, except..." Faison pointed to Raimond. "When I asked that one if he wanted to live, he said yes."

"A heinous trick!" Raimond lodged the burly guard's neck in the crook of his elbow. Skull and spine separated with the thunder of a tree splitting in a storm. He grabbed the soldier's gold dagger and zoomed at Faison. "Why? Why me?"

"Your choice. I'll tell you that particular secret—" Faison grabbed Aveline's hair with a vicious twist and crushed the muzzle of a pistol to her temple, "—for this precious angel's life."

Aveline arched her back and drove her heel into Faison's chest.

"Kick me again, little wench." Faison spun her around and smashed the back of her skull into iron bars. He stopped to wait for her howl and kept going until her hand released the dagger.

"Kill him, Raimond!" Aveline kneed him in the groin. "Behind you, Parlan!"

The thin guards came back to life and pointed their swords at Parlan's chest.

"That was quick," Parlan grunted. "We should have gone for the hearts."

"Mistakes will forever return to haunt us." Faison's finger flinched on the trigger and his eyes flared with red fire. "But my soldiers don't need gold to cut the Scot's chest wide open."

"You're despicable, using a girl as a shield." Raimond sliced the burly guard's head off with his stolen dagger. "That's likely permanent."

Faison cringed at Raimond's bold step in his direction. "I'll put a gold bullet in your sister's head before you can blink."

Aveline closed her eyes as Faison squeezed the trigger. Time stood still.

"His glove!" Parlan took one guard out at the knees. "Jammed in the trigger!"

The last guard left drove his sword into Parlan's shoulder. Faison threw Aveline to the ground, stepped on her neck and chambered another bullet.

Raimond held up both hands but didn't let go of the dagger. He slid back and pounded on the cell door. "Anton, Siras—open up!"

Echoes of a hammer on the iron bar filled the prison chamber. At the second the door creaked open, Faison and his men broke free, knocking Anton and Siras into the far wall.

"Raimond, gold!" Aveline flashed to his side, grabbed the blade from his hand and hurled it at their fleeing captors. Faison and one of his guards escaped, unharmed. The other fell to the floor with Aveline's dagger in his back.

"Parlan!" Raimond clamped his hands on his friend's wound. "This didn't go as planned."

"It was steel." Parlan pushed him away. "I barely felt it."

"That was some throw." Anton rolled the guard over to find a gold tip protruding from his chest. "Bloody magnificent, Aveline."

Siras joined his brother, trying to yank the blade free. It didn't budge. "Must be in his heart."

Raimond kicked the body aside. "We have to go after them!"

Parlan seized weapons dropped by the guards and tossed them to Anton and Siras. "Grab your gear, men!"

A tiny voice squeaked from the corner. "What about us?"

"They can't fight or chase villains, Raimond." Aveline nodded to children cowering in the corner. "They're terrified of disappointing you."

"They stay here." Raimond found an elderly woman struggling with her coat. He took her frail hands in his and softened his voice. "You too, *madame*. Remember the new ways I've been teaching? Be kind and be safe. We'll come back for you."

"Let's move." Parlan hauled Raimond away. "We'll lose the scent."

"The Commander always keeps his promises." Aveline patted a trembling girl's shoulder on her way out. She climbed over the dead guard, stopped and retraced her steps. She nudged the grey flesh with her foot and his fingers fell to ash. The gold dagger dislodged in her grasp as the rest of the corpse disintegrated.

The room full of little vampires clapped and cheered for Aveline as she bowed and ran up the steps.

Chapter 7
SPELLS & TREASURES

RAIMOND SNIFFED THE air as they chased Faison through the labyrinth of Paris alleys. The first time he lost the scent, Aveline crouched down to cracked cobblestones and chanted a few words.

"That way." She pointed south to a crooked lane, stood and stumbled.

"What was that?" Anton grabbed her arm. "Latin?"

Aveline giggled. "Maybe."

The next time the group found themselves at an unmarked crossroads, they fanned out in all possible directions. Each vampire returned to the intersection shaking their head and Parlan dropped to the ground, pressing his ear to the grime. "I hear nothing."

Aveline stepped beside him and chanted again, in a language no one recognized. "Follow the dirty water." She coughed, covered her mouth and wound up with two handfuls of blood.

"Aveline," Siras hissed. "You're getting sicker!"

"It's nothing new." Aveline pressed her finger to her lips. "Don't distract Raimond."

By the time they reached the outskirts of the city, Anton and Siras were taking turns carrying her.

"I'm weighing you down." Aveline pounded on Anton's chest. "Leave me behind."

"Here?" Anton looked at his feet. The bridge under him wobbled over a stream that smelled of rotten eggs.

"We need you, *mademoiselle*." Raimond flashed back and hoisted her onto his shoulder. "Light as a feather."

Siras jogged to keep up with Raimond's fast walk. "Aveline, where did you learn the odd spells and spooky stuff?"

She forced her tired eyes open and gave a brief smile. "Wouldn't you love to know?"

"Didn't you see her kill that bad man?" Anton ran beside Siras and punched his shoulder. "That girl might be tougher than you."

Aveline waved them off with frail fingers and let her chin rest on Raimond's shoulder.

Parlan and Raimond shared the role of leading the chase. Glowing lights of Paris disappeared long before dawn's first rays threatened the horizon. With Faison's scent still vibrating in the air, they were forced to take refuge under an abandoned barn.

"They must be hiding close by." Parlan slammed a splintering hatch shut behind him and crawled around stray beams of sunlight on his way to the back of the room.

"They definitely picked up reinforcements outside the city wall." Raimond discovered a trunk of tattered clothes and handed them out. He tucked a heavy coat around Aveline and himself. "Keep hidden. This old building has cracks."

"Write in the magic books." Aveline snuggled under Raimond's arm. "You too, Parlan."

"About what, dear?" Parlan fumbled in his pocket.

"Your parents, the homeless man. Everything we survive together—" Aveline screeched.

Raimond flinched back. "What?"

"I saw it again." She pointed to Raimond's eyes. "The silhouettes!"

"Shhh!" He clamped his hand over her mouth. "What are you talking about?"

She pushed his hand away. "In my family's bible—"

"The grimoire?" Parlan asked.

Aveline nodded. "From what I could decipher, the shadows are outlines of crypts."

Raimond groaned and cleared his throat. "Go on."

"Apparently, it's the sign of a soul who is in tune with both sides of the veil. The living and the dead." Aveline held out her hands. "The past and the future."

"Sounds like a curse." Parlan sighed.

"Or an incredible power." Raimond tucked the coat tighter around them. "Does this miracle have a name?"

"I could barely read it and the rest of the grimoire was burned. Or covered in blood."

Raimond rested his chin on her head. "Lovely."

"You might not want to hear this…" Aveline buried her face in his neck. "But I definitely saw something about bones."

At dusk, the chase continued through dense forests and boggy valleys. Raimond had to look twice before he trusted his eyes, but with every mile they traveled, radiant hues of green and pink replaced Paris' blue, black and grey of despair. At a line of blooming fruit trees, Faison's scent grew faint until it disappeared at a mill nestled in a swell of long grass. Just beyond the stone walls, silver water swirled around a sharp bend and reflected hints of the clouded moon above.

"I must have lost my bearings." Parlan looked at the stars and stared at the rushing water. "The river, could it be—"

"The Loire?" Raimond peered behind Parlan at the twinkling lights of a village. "Then we would be just south of Orleans."

"I see a bridge." Parlan pointed downriver. Plumes of frost rose from ghostly rapids. "The scent leads that way."

"Too dangerous. Could be a trap." Raimond turned his back on civilization. "We'll have to swim."

"I can't," Siras pulled Anton beside him. "Neither can—"

"Chunks of ice are floating out there." Anton's eyes bulged. "We'll sink like stones."

"You will not." Raimond yanked the door of the mill open and scanned the dark interior.

"That's what we need." Parlan marched past and grabbed lengths of rope. He handed one coil to Anton and the other to Siras. "Tie yourselves together."

Aveline held her open hand out to Parlan. "I'll take both books and keep them dry."

"I thought you spelled them." Parlan dug his from an inside pocket.

"I did, the writing…against magic." Aveline presented her other palm to Raimond. "Wet leather is just soggy."

"Look at these two." Parlan rolled his eyes at Anton and Siras as they fumbled with the rope. He shooed them back and tightened the knots until the strands were fused. "I'll drag them across."

"I've got the lady." Raimond hoisted Aveline onto his shoulders and waded into the river first, battling the current with powerful strokes.

"Stop!" Aveline beat on his head. "Wait!"

"What?" Raimond paused and immediately got sucked back toward the river's center. "We were almost there."

"They're pulling Parlan down!" Aveline pointed to dark figures in the churning water. "We have to go back!"

In seconds, Raimond and Aveline were close enough to join hands with Parlan.

"Keep going!" Parlan waved them off.

"No, no! Siras went under!" Aveline flailed, lost her balance and landed with a splash and a shriek.

"Aveline!" Raimond lunged, but the river swept her beyond his outstretched reach. "Parlan, grab her!"

"Hold this." He tossed the waterlogged rope to Raimond and dove for Aveline. "You're stronger than me, anyway."

Raimond only began swimming for the far bank after she was safely in Parlan's arms. He dug his heels into muddy gravel and hauled the struggling twins ashore.

Anton flopped onto his back with a coarse gasp, and slapped Siras between the shoulder blades.

"We made it!" Aveline jumped off Parlan's back and held the books high over her head. "And these never went under."

"Yes, but your whole head did." Raimond held her face in his hands. "And your lips are blue."

Parlan crossed his arms and shook his head as Siras gagged up a lungful of water. "Scotland is full of lakes. Whatever county you two lads are from, not sure how you survived."

"The chill has her again." Raimond searched in vain for something to dry Aveline off. "She needs to feed."

"We all do." Parlan emptied his dripping pockets. "Don't suppose anyone has dry matches?"

"Not even one." Aveline's shivering grew into violent tremors. "Hopefully, when we find shelter, we'll find fire too."

The clan zipped across fields and ducked into the barn of an ivy-draped manor house. Behind an imposing well-oiled door, warmth and the scent of livestock embraced them like a blanket.

"These animals have strong blood, but it may not be enough." Siras brushed shards of ice out of his red hair. He took a few steps toward a dappled grey horse before Raimond redirected him to a cow. He groaned and gagged. "We definitely need more than that lowly beast."

Muffled kicks of hooves on stall walls ignited nervous whinnies that echoed through the building.

"Parlan, take the men and Aveline to the house. It looks cozy but not extravagant enough to have sentries." Raimond stepped to the left of the muscular stallion and held out his hand to set the creature at ease. "I know strength is essential to keep up this pursuit, but I expect everyone to follow the new rules."

"You're going to drink from the horses, sir?" Anton rubbed the base of his neck. "Because animal blood alone—"

"We may need to ride them." Raimond waved the men off and pulled a folded paper out of his pocket. "Hurry back. Dawn won't wait." While his companions hunted, he pored over an old map, tracing the river with his finger. By the time they returned, he was pounding his forehead with his fist.

"Are you unwell?" Aveline tapped his shoulder. "I found a friend who can help. She's a healer too."

"No dear, I'm just—" Raimond's jaw quivered at the sight of the strawberry blonde holding Aveline's hand. "You shouldn't have brought her here. We all agreed that children were off limits."

"Oh no Commander, you've misunderstood." The girl flicked her hand through the air, leaving a trail of stars bright enough to illuminate the dark barn. "Nobody has fed from me. I drink the silver sage potion every morning."

"*Désolé,*" Raimond mumbled and forced himself to speak English. "I apologize. You'll need to explain."

"Let me help." Parlan strode to the middle of the barn. "This Scottish lass is Kaleigh, the kitchen maid. She has an herb that repels vampires. Do you not smell it?"

Raimond inhaled and flinched. "Sour, bitter, foul…can't pinpoint it. Wait, she knows—"

"Of course, I do. The road we live on is a main thoroughfare for your kind." Kaleigh pointed into the darkness. "I don't adore the family I work for, but they do pay me and we all need protection."

"So, no one has fed?" Raimond slumped against a polished timber. "Faison's scent is fading every second we waste here."

"There's more." Parlan tapped Kaleigh's shoulder. "Tell him."

"The silver sage is a family secret, but easily grown. The original plants are from a castle in Wales where my great-grandmother worked for years."

"Keep going." Siras stirred the air with his fingers. "All of it, don't be shy."

"Well," she rubbed both hands on her crisp apron, "I keep these snobby French people alive, but I also put them to sleep when they get in my way."

"She's a witch." Aveline skimmed her hand through sparks which still hung in the air. "A real one and she's on our side."

"We're fighting for our lives." Raimond's eyes landed on Kaleigh. "But it's family business and much too dangerous for a young girl, witch or otherwise."

"Are you not hungry?" Kaleigh looked around to see everyone nod in unison. "I have skills to trade."

"You do realize what…" Raimond crossed his arms. "You must be desperate for something."

"I'll provide humans to feed on, as long as you aren't murderers."

"We are not," Parlan assured her. "Raimond is forging a new civilization."

"I'm sure you lost the trail when you jumped in the river." Kaleigh wrapped her coat around Aveline's quaking shoulders. "Luckily, I know where the Paris villain and his gang hide."

Raimond's eyes lit up. "That changes everything."

"I only ask one favor in return."

"Changing you into a monster is out of the question." Raimond spun to face a wall of oiled tack and polished buckles. "You're too young. Much too young."

"Oh, dear Lord, no." Kaleigh covered her eyes. "Just help me escape wretched France and go home."

"Home," Parlan mumbled. "Home."

"In that case," Raimond turned back just enough to look her up and down, "I give you my word."

Parlan touched Kaleigh's shoulder. "His word is treasure."

Chapter 8

SACRIFICE

BEHIND BROCADE AND tasseled curtains long enough to pool on the floor, the vampires quenched their thirst in the brick manor. After they were finished, Raimond checked that every scar was healed, while Parlan rearranged the lady of the house's waterfall of delicate braids on her shoulders.

"I know you claimed to be different, but I can't believe—" Kaleigh flung her hands in the air. "Who are you again?"

"That's a good question." Parlan glanced at Raimond. "Are we Clan Banitierre?"

"Not yet," Raimond meticulously re-inspected each bite. "We'll choose a name after our future is assured."

"Well, the first step to setting your destiny is defeating the enemy. Fighting takes strength. Strength requires blood." Kaleigh pulled empty bottles from a painted ivory cupboard. "Only simple magic is necessary to create blood-wine. You don't even need good wine."

"Or good blood." Aveline met Kaleigh's eyes and both girls broke into a fit of giggles.

At Kaleigh's direction, Anton and Siras dragged a leather-bound trunk from the manor's basement and plunked it next to a fire pit outside the kitchen door. She whistled three notes and flames burst to life inside the ring of etched stones. "Anyone still thirsty?"

The question was met with silent nods and a sea of wide eyes.

Kaleigh opened the trunk lid, pulled out a bottle and poured wine into a metal cup. "Vintage, one hour."

Raimond sampled it first. "Not bad." He handed the cup to Parlan.

Parlan swallowed and passed it to Siras. "That will be heavenly when we're starving."

"No reason to go hungry anymore." Kaleigh handed a full bottle to Raimond, motioning for everyone to slide closer while she found a twig and drew a map in the dirt. "The bad vampires aren't far from here." She scratched a curvy line into the ground. "Those are hills."

Parlan hunched forward. "How far away?"

"Five miles." Kaleigh tapped her stick on the ground. "And a few more to travel on the other side before your destination, but don't panic. You'll have the horses until the edge of the forest."

"What are you drawing now?" Aveline crouched next to Kaleigh. "Little houses?"

"No." Kaleigh outlined a large box under the many pointy roofs. "A castle."

Anton inched closer. "That's all one building?"

"Yes, it's garish," Kaleigh said. "And so poorly planned, that even kings don't want to live there."

Raimond stood and peered over their shoulders. "Chambord."

"You know it?" Kaleigh asked.

"By reputation." Raimond crossed his arms. "Is it truly a madman's maze?"

"It is." Kaleigh held up a glass vial of murky liquid. "But you won't get lost. I'll make sure you can track the villain's scent, no matter where they hide on the property."

"We'll need a battle plan." Parlan looked at the crew of four men and Aveline. "And an advantage."

Kaleigh pulled a rough grey bag from a pocket in the trunk's lid. "I can cloak you just long enough to cross the open field, but it expires when you pass the threshold."

Parlan nodded. "One major hurdle eliminated."

"Yet, there are so many more." Kaleigh fished around in the trunk until she found a silver box. "I'll need the best weapon you possess. Doesn't need to be gold, just something with a personal connection."

Raimond shook his head at the sword that hung from his belt. "All I've got is a piece of rubbish stolen from…them."

Parlan sighed and unsheathed a dagger. "This is Damascus steel, smuggled into the Highlands by my grandfather."

"Perfect." Kaleigh took it, tested the weight in her hands and examined the initials *P L* carved in the handle. "An heirloom?"

"If you have to melt it," Parlan took the blade back and swallowed hard, "I'll understand."

"Oh heavens, no." Kaleigh patted her chest. "I'll spell it into a dark object, capable of killing any vampire with one blow. Only catch is you can never change it back."

Raimond glanced at Parlan with a shrug. "That's up to you, brother. It's your family heritage."

"We're outmanned." Parlan ran his finger over the razor-sharp tip. "I'll sacrifice it."

"This spell requires time to take hold, so we need to do it now." Kaleigh found a bowl carved from bone and set it next to the fire. She waved her hand over the silver box until the lid popped open. Inside, a black streaked egg sat cushioned in velvet.

"Do we want to know what creature laid that thing?" Anton asked.

"Doubt it." Kaleigh held her breath and lifted the egg over the bowl. She nodded to Parlan. "Crack the shell with the blade."

The egg broke cleanly.

"I've seen a lot of eggs." Raimond blinked hard. "Never a black yolk."

"I need the blood of the leader." Kaleigh exhaled and gripped the dagger.

Raimond looked for Parlan's approval before holding his hand over the bowl. He winced as the knife sliced through his skin and hit bone. "Almost took my fingers off."

"Sorry, it's sharper than I thought." Kaleigh lifted the final item, a brown spice stick, from the silver box. She lit at the edge of the fire pit.

Aveline raised her nose and sniffed. "Clove?"

"If you recognize it, Aveline, then I think you'll love this spell." Kaleigh mumbled unintelligible words with Scottish flair and plunged the smoking clove stick into the center of the yolk.

Siras recoiled. "Smells dreadful."

"Just wait." Kaleigh wiggled her fingers before plunging one hand into the smoldering brew. "Hot, hot."

Anton and Parlan shrank away as Kaleigh smeared bloody black egg up and down the wavy design forged into the steel of the dagger. She nicked her finger and shrieked but kept working until the entire surface was coated with clotted magic goop.

Aveline leaned closer.

Kaleigh waved her clean hand behind her. "Hand me the chain mail."

Aveline rushed to the trunk and dug around until she held up a dirty mass of woven metal. She frowned. "It's pretty tarnished."

"It's ancient." Kaleigh wrapped the blade in tight rings of sterling silver. "Not one drop of grease on the hilt. Now, it needs to cook."

Raimond crept away from the fire before unfolding the tattered map in his pocket. He turned it upside down, dragging his finger along the crude line of the river, rotating the picture side to side to get his bearings. "Ah, now I understand where we are."

"I'll prepare spells and find donors to make more wine during the day while you rest." Kaleigh wiped her hands on her apron and leaned into the trunk. Silence made her straighten up with a scowl. "The sun is almost up. You'll be protected in the well house." She jabbed her thumb at a gloomy stone building. "Go!"

One by one, the vampires filed away. Raimond waited until they were gone and turned to Kaleigh. "You've been in that castle?"

"Several times, though I was most likely trespassing."

The corner of Raimond's mouth drifted up. "Thank you again, for helping us and for feeding my little family."

"My pleasure. I can't wait to be away from this miserable country for good."

"I used to think France was the pinnacle of enlightened civilization. That was a grave mistake."

"What used to be beautiful has become the land of death and misery." Kaleigh put her hand to her cheek and swiped a tear. "I miss Scotland."

Raimond knelt and squeezed her hand in his. "I promise, if we survive, we won't leave you behind."

"You'll do more than survive, kind sir." Kaleigh raised her free hand to his face. "My magic will bring you glorious triumph."

In the misty pre-dawn glow, Raimond lingered before the dirt drawing of Chambord. He dragged the heel of his boot through the center of the towers before flashing to the dark safety of the well house.

Chapter 9

WOLVES OF THE LOIRE

AFTER THE SUN made its lazy descent below the horizon, Kaleigh supervised the bridling of horses and packing of fancy saddlebags.

"Kaleigh, are those—" Aveline peeked through tiny cracks in the barn wall and staggered. "Dogs?"

"Oh, excellent!" Kaleigh twisted a scrolled key and threw all her weight against the massive door until it rolled back. "My messenger succeeded."

"Those are wolves." Anton backed away and shoved Siras in front of him.

"Kaleigh?" Raimond pulled Aveline behind him. "What's the plan?"

"Yes, they're wolves." Kaleigh patted each of the five animals on the head. "But very different from the myths you've been told."

Siras thrashed both hands in front of his face. "It's still a bloody curse."

"As is ours." Aveline broke from Raimond's grasp and held her hand out for the closest wolf. The massive red beast sniffed her hand and perked up its ears.

Parlan glanced at the moon. "Not full...I don't understand."

"Luck is on our side." Kaleigh waved the men back to their preparations. "We need animals for protection, not humans."

Aveline shook her head. "I'm dying of curiosity."

"This pack's curse, if you're set on calling it that, is triggered on every fifth child's twentieth birthday."

"Girls, too?" Aveline's eyes widened.

"Oh, yes." Kaleigh smiled and walked over to the smallest wolf. She ruffled the silvery blue fur around her ears. "All the rest have shed their human names, but this is Perette."

Aveline knelt. "Pleased to meet you, Miss Perette.

The little blue wolf licked Aveline's face cautiously and then leapt into her arms like a joyful puppy. The men groaned.

Kaleigh went back to work saddling her horse. "By midnight of the occasion, each child must decide whether they want to change to wolf form during full moons, or the opposite."

"So, they turn back to human for one night a month?" Raimond's gaze drifted to the hazy treeline. "What an odd choice."

"The four boys were childhood friends whose birthdays fell within the same week. He's the alpha." Kaleigh pointed to the red giant, and then at Perette. "She only turned twenty last year."

"Quite an adjustment in lifestyle." Anton eyed a wolf with fur as black as his own floppy curls.

"A sound decision at the time they changed," Kaleigh said. "The first shots of the Revolution had been fired."

"Yes." Parlan stared at Raimond. "We remember."

"Back then, food was becoming scarce for humans." Kaleigh made a final check of the girth and climbed onto her horse. "Now that the royal reserves have been hunted to near extinction, food isn't plentiful for wolves either."

"Aren't their bites lethal?" Raimond swung onto the grey stallion's back and held the beast still until Aveline was seated behind him. "To us, I mean?"

The final three mounted and waited for Kaleigh's explanation.

"It's an important point." Anton pointed to wolves pacing the barnyard. "Aren't we their arch enemies?"

"Not this pack." Kaleigh nudged her horse ahead into an open field. "That's the other unique thing about their curse...their choice of nemesis was not vampires."

All faces turned to her. The horses came to an uneasy halt and the wolf pack glided to a silent stop.

"It's witches." Kaleigh sighed and transferred the reins to one hand. The wolves milled in a tight circle, never taking their yellow eyes off her. She nodded to each one until they stood still. "I've built a friendship with these five, but their bites are still instantly fatal to me and my kind."

Kaleigh kicked her horse and took off across the moonlit grass.

Raimond urged his stallion to keep pace as she faded in and out of wispy mist. "How does this help us then?"

"Patience, you'll see." Kaleigh pointed to the foothills. A few minutes of galloping brought the group to shadows where the land began to rise.

Aveline whispered in Raimond's ear, "I smell lemons."

Kaleigh reined in her horse the second before sentries bearing Faison's scorpion insignia leapt out and blocked the trail.

"Here we go!" Parlan's horse slid to a stop and he leapt to the ground, legs churning. "Anton! Siras! I'll snap their necks. You boys, slice off their heads!" ·

With Parlan still charging, lupine predators lunged from both sides. With snapping jaws and pinpoint accuracy, the first two wolves blasted upward, under their target's ribs. The next beasts hit from the opposite direction, each clamping onto a guard's skull, twisting and driving the vampires to the ground.

Anton and Siras drew their swords in full stride and sliced off the guards' heads simultaneously.

Parlan looked over his shoulder with a chuckle. "I almost feel left out."

"You? I never took my feet out of the stirrups." Raimond shrugged. "Our wolf friends did make things simpler."

"Indeed." Parlan swung back into the saddle. "And I think they have a taste for it."

The wolves circled the disintegrating corpses. The red giant licked blood from his lips and threw his head back. A wicked howl echoed across the valley.

"Not immediate death to vampires like legends tell, but the damage they can inflict..." Kaleigh steered her horse toward a wall of green. She ducked under low branches in a hidden gap. The head of a trail was marked with bizarre faces painted on tree trunks. "Definitely an advantage."

Raimond urged the grey stallion to charge up the steep path. Aveline squeezed his waist tighter while pounding hooves mimicked what he remembered of his heartbeat. A cadence long gone.

Kaleigh reigned her horse in at the top of the hill. She pushed the hood of her cloak back and let her hair whip in the wind.

"Are we there yet?" Aveline peeked past Raimond's shoulder as his mount slowed and snorted.

One at a time, horses skidded to a stop on the ridge. Each rider's jaw dropped as the moon emerged from behind clouds and lit the scene below. Centered in the lush valley like a crown jewel, the prickly silhouette of a massive chateau emerged, one mismatched spire at a time.

"Some people have a lot of money to waste," Parlan chuckled.

"Royals," Siras grunted. "All the same, no matter what country they're from."

"Looks spooky," Anton said. "And abandoned."

"I saw it all lit up." Kaleigh held her prancing mount steady. "But only once, for a summer party."

"Bad news." Aveline pointed to horses and a carriage pulling up under an arch in the massive wall. "More henchmen."

"We'll stay hidden in the woods as long as possible and sneak in through a canal that feeds the moat." Kaleigh gestured to the northwest corner. "The windows are broken in that tower."

Raimond nudged his horse next to Kaleigh. "You don't have to accompany us. You've done enough and it's dangerous."

"If Aveline is going," Kaleigh called over her shoulder, "then I'm going."

Raimond motioned for the others to follow. As the trail narrowed to a torturous winding path, tree branches slashed his face like a wave of needles. He slowed only when Aveline whimpered in pain.

At the bottom of the hill, Kaleigh dismounted and held her hand up to keep everyone under the forest's camouflage. She dug into her saddlebag until she found a sachet of teeth and dried flowers, along with an overripe lemon. "For you, Aveline. Remember what to do?"

Aveline fished a knife from her pocket. "Slice it up."

Kaleigh turned her back to the castle and lit the flowers and teeth mixture in a small crucible.

Anton held his nose.

Kaleigh snuffed the flame and lifted the iron pot high enough to waft around everyone's head. "Like it or not, you need to breathe it."

"Oh, hell." Siras coughed and forced himself to inhale. "Smells like burnt hair and rotten bananas."

"Choke it down, men." Raimond clapped Anton and Siras on the back. "It makes you invisible."

When the crucible held nothing but fine ash, Kaleigh blew it in the direction of the open field. "Aveline, did you cut the lemon?"

"Six pieces." Aveline held out the wedges.

"It won't work for me, just vampires." Kaleigh pulled the murky vial out of her coat pocket and dripped liquid onto each wedge. "Every time those bandits tear past our house, the air is heavy with citrus."

"I smelled that, right before the ambush." Aveline nodded. "Just couldn't identify it."

"I've enhanced it." Kaleigh coughed into her sleeve. "Hopefully not too much."

"What do we do with these?" Anton shrugged at Siras.

"Suck the juice out." Kaleigh pushed Raimond's wedge toward his mouth. "With a little luck, it will mask your scent from other vampires just long enough to give you the upper hand."

Raimond followed her instructions, failing to hide an involuntary gag.

Parlan laughed and held his piece up. "Like the Commander said, choke it down men."

Aveline drained her lemon wedge dry. Her fingers squashed the rind into yellow pulp as she wandered to the edge of the oaks and sniffed the breeze. "Oh, yes." Her eyes scanned the field and zeroed in on the castle. "They're in there. A whole lot of them."

The men finished their tasks, traded sour faces and tossed the cut fruit away.

Raimond wiped his mouth and shuddered. "I'll never look at lemon the same again. But Aveline is right. The smell from that chateau is like a royal orchard on fire."

"The moon has risen high." Parlan rubbed his palms together. "We need to get started."

"Leave the horses loose." Kaleigh patted her mare's neck. "They'll stay until they get hungry. By then, we should be—will be back."

The group of six picked their way along the river's edge until they found a narrow canal. The cut stone wall ended at the base of a white tower.

"This window is not broken." Parlan's gaze drifted higher up the wall. "But that one is missing entirely."

"Someone has been here working on the grounds." Raimond's gaze darted back to the sculptured garden and dark caretaker's sheds. "Breaking glass will draw too much attention. We need to climb into the second floor."

"I'm not cloaked anymore." Aveline jumped across the black water and started scaling the limestone.

"Wait! You can't—" Raimond leapt onto the wall and climbed past her. "*Mademoiselle*, these men are killers."

"Staying out in the open is not an option," Aveline hissed. She pointed to the window. "Move!"

Raimond peeked into the wide opening before hoisting himself into the dark chamber. He hauled both girls in and held his finger to his lips while the men joined him. The faint clink of bottles and commotion of a party echoed deep in the mansion.

"I hear Faison," Raimond growled. "I'd recognize that voice anywhere."

"They must be in an interior suite." Kaleigh peered down the hall. "But there are so many windows and glass ceilings, they'll hide in the basement during the day."

"How do we get there?" Anton crept into the open until a little hand grabbed his coat.

"Not the main stairs. You'd get lost for sure." Kaleigh motioned for everyone to follow. "Hidden servant's passageway."

On the splintered wooden steps, lingering lemon battled the musty aroma of emptiness, growing fainter as they traveled farther away from Faison. Below ground level, Raimond brushed the dusty wall, finding rough foundation underneath. With a flint from his pocket, he lit a small torch and turned in a circle. Each corridor that fanned out under the castle began with a meticulously carved pillar and ended in churning black oblivion. He brushed his ears imagining a wall of cobwebs.

"We'll find the space with the strongest scent and ambush them." Parlan struck a second torch, sniffed the air and followed his nose to a round chamber. Makeshift beds lined the walls and blood red sconces cast an eerie glow in every direction. Under the unfinished ceiling of sharp stone fragments, a polished box overflowed with extravagant linen. "More damn tunnels."

"I thought this was a joke." Anton leaned closer to Siras' ear. "Didn't you?"

Siras shoved him away. "Nothing about this entire situation has been funny."

"Apparently, the legend is true. Our sire sleeps in a coffin." Raimond's eyes snapped red and then pure black. Aside from maddening whispers he had initially mistaken for cobwebs, the silence was only broken by his muddy boots hitting stone. Without a word he tore velvet and satin to ribbons. When the elegant curves of the coffin were reduced to gleaming splinters, he took a deep breath, closed his eyes and spit on the wreckage. "I'm going to plant that bloody wicked bastard in it for eternity."

Chapter 10

THE RHYTHM OF TIME

AFTER GOING OVER their attack plan twice, five vampires and one witch settled in to their shadowy hiding places for a third rehearsal. Voices in the darkest tunnel made them freeze.

"It's not even dawn." Parlan snuffed his torch and let the ambient glow take over. His wide eyes found Raimond. "Move to the next passage!"

Raimond flashed around the corner and flattened his back against the wall. His hand slipped to the sheath on his belt and his fingers clutched empty air. "Wait, where's my—Kaleigh, the knife!"

"I wasn't ready." Kaleigh slapped her forehead and ran for a bag resting near the coffin.

Aveline yanked her back. "You'll never get there in time."

Raimond swiveled toward ominous footsteps that fell like gunshots, growing louder by the second. Aveline landed in his arms with the dagger still wrapped in chain mail. They both clamped a hand over each other's mouth to stay silent.

Parlan flailed his arms in the air until Raimond set Aveline aside.

Raimond shrugged and Parlan held up three fingers.

"Only three?" Raimond whispered. He pointed at Anton and Siras in their respective tunnels. "Remember the plan."

The words of the enemy transformed the hushed chamber into a ring of rage.

"I need peace and quiet." Faison stormed in, stopped and charged back at his two bodyguards. "Your friends upstairs—drunken fools!"

"They're angry about our brothers being murdered." The tall guard clenched his fists. "By lowly slaves."

"They're angry? I should have fired the lot. They should be mortified at their own incompetence. And if they don't wake up by dawn in that atrium, they'll be cooked like…" Faison stared at his ruined coffin. "What the hell happened in here?"

Raimond's eyes throbbed inside their sockets. He squeezed Aveline's bony arm and gave her his sternest look.

Parlan tossed a ring of keys into the coffin and the ambush exploded. Faison spun around in time to see Anton and Siras pounce on his guards.

"What is the meaning of this?" Faison charged.

Raimond appeared in front of him like a torchlit specter. "Payback."

Anton grabbed his guard's head, latching onto the big man's ears like handles. He dodged one flying elbow and twisted the bald skull. The second elbow caught him in the jaw, but a final burst of power twisted the guard's head almost backward and the man dropped to the dust with a choked grunt. Anton's attention shot to Siras.

In the mouth of the farthest tunnel, a lanky guard pinned Siras against the wall by the neck. Anton leapt onto the man's back and all three crashed to the floor. When the guard drew his fist back to punch Siras, Anton stole the sword from his belt. Siras ducked and the guard changed direction, striking the sword from Anton's hand with a perfect kick.

Siras lunged for the enemy's neck but the man was ready, and effortlessly slammed Siras' face into a stone pillar.

The guard beat his own chest like a warrior and reclaimed his weapon. "Let's go, boss."

"I think not." Raimond forced himself between Faison and the guard. He drove the heel of his boot into the eye of the squirming soldier on the floor.

When the tall guard bolted into the darkness, Anton grabbed a groggy Siras and followed.

"You seem to be alone, Faison." Raimond crossed his arms. "Unprotected, like a sitting duck."

Faison wheeled to the far tunnel.

Parlan blocked his path. "If you had webbed feet, they'd be broken."

"His feathers would be shredded." Raimond surprised himself and revealed an evil grin.

Aveline flashed to Raimond's side. "His fowl heart is already cold?"

Raimond laughed like a maniac.

"You're all idiots." Faison grabbed his head and pivoted to see wolves closing in. "And these beasts you've brought are worthless."

"We will see." Parlan held his arms out. "You're trapped."

Every direction Faison turned was blocked by a vampire, witch or wolf. Perette bared her teeth and Faison made a false lunge. The little wolf waited for him to retreat and then sprung, sinking her fangs into Faison's thigh. His shrieks made her clamp down tighter, tearing a jagged hole in his flesh.

"Perette, look out!" Aveline rushed forward.

Faison grabbed an unlit torch from the wall, clubbed the little wolf's skull and fled down the tunnel with the rest of the pack on his heels.

Aveline scooped Perette in her arms as the others raced past, chasing the limping Faison. "Raimond, wait!"

Raimond flashed back to find Aveline holding her ear to the wolf's chest. "No heartbeat?"

Aveline shook her head. "Try a few drops of your blood...so much stronger than mine."

"On an animal?"

"Please, she's special."

Raimond nicked his wrist and held it over the wolf's head wound.

Aveline redirected Raimond's arm and sunk to the ground. "On her tongue." She coaxed little jaws open with her fingers and massaged the limp animal's throat with practiced hands.

Raimond vanished into the darkness to rejoin the chase. Under silver moonlight warped by wavy glass, he found Faison lighting furnishings on fire and making steady progress toward the spiral staircase at the castle's center.

"You can't escape." Raimond flung his arms wide. "And I'm not afraid of fire."

The wall of flames looked daunting but burned out quickly as it consumed the fuel. Amidst the floor and walls of solid stone, Parlan, Anton and Siras closed in. Raimond struggled to maintain eye contact with the enemy.

Faison kicked burning furniture forward, edged towards the stairs and jumped through the blaze.

"Damn it!" Parlan flashed to the edge of the flames.

Raimond backed up a few steps and followed Faison through the inferno. His ears registered Aveline's screams and shouts from his men as he shed his coat and beat the flickers in his hair to submission. Footsteps echoed up and down the double helix staircase. He started down and changed his mind, running back to where he began.

Through the dying fire, Kaleigh pointed up.

"*Merci.*" Raimond bounded up multiple steps at a time, following the bitter trail of lemons. At the first landing guards raced toward him from a courtyard of roses choked by weeds. He paused for a second until wolves burst from the darkness and drove the vampires back into the thorns.

Aveline slammed the door and locked the vampires in. "Nothing in their minds but murder."

Kaleigh caught up, motioned for Raimond to continue and intercepted Anton and Siras. "Mind the second staircase."

"The what?" Siras looked helplessly at the walls until Kaleigh dragged him halfway around the hulking stone spiral.

"There are two completely separate stair structures. You can be on one and never meet people on the other."

"We'll take this one." Anton held out his torch and Kaleigh lit it with a touch.

"Keep moving!" Parlan charged past Raimond. "He's working himself into a corner."

At the next landing, Raimond stopped and pressed his fingers to his lips. He motioned Parlan to the opposite side of the corridor. They found Faison trapped on a bed frame, in a chamber strewn with relics fit for a king. Leering mahogany gargoyles faced off against a pack of drooling wolves.

"Call off your dogs, Banitierre." Faison brushed back the moth-eaten canopy. "Fight me, monster to monster."

Parlan whispered in Raimond's ear. "Remember the spelled blade."

"*Oui.*" Raimond held his hand up to halt the wolves. "Let's settle this, once and for all."

Kaleigh and Aveline appeared right before Anton and Siras rushed into the room.

"I do so love an audience." Faison leapt, landing in the center of the spectators.

"Leg looks bad." Raimond unsheathed his curved French sword.

Faison grimaced and forced himself to stand straight. "Is that all you brought?"

"I'm a soldier." Raimond twirled the bulky military blade like a wand of feathers. "Weapon of choice."

"It's your farewell performance." Faison's eyes fell on Parlan's unassuming dagger. He chuckled, pulled out his gun and tossed away his gloves. "No misfires this time."

"Those hands!" Aveline gasped. "His skin looks burned or dead."

"Just to make it more entertaining." Faison dropped all but one gold bullet from the barrel of the revolver and tossed the weapon to his other hand. "For me, anyway."

"You're insane." Raimond motioned everyone back and crouched for the attack.

"I'm your sire." Faison pulled out his own gold blade and lunged. "Don't ever forget it."

"Is that all you have?" Raimond sprung forward, but Faison evaded his sword.

"Hardly." Faison leapt again, this time slicing Raimond's cheek with his blade.

The circle of wolves growled and tightened their formation.

"It will take far more than that to stop me." Raimond dabbed blood from his cheek and grinned at his friends. "He's a coward."

"I found you as a crumpled corpse." Faison's red eyes glinted black in the center. "I made you and your weak little followers."

"Should I be grateful?" Raimond tipped his head.

Faison sprung forward and Raimond mirrored his attack, striking the blade from the villain's hand and sending it clattering across the floorboards.

Aveline and Faison grabbed for the gold. The giant red wolf slammed Faison back, tearing the sleeve off his right arm.

"Mine." Aveline clutched the dagger. "Oh ick, his arms are charred too."

Faison's face fell dark, starting at his eyes and blasting across his cheeks. "I've had enough of all of you." He raised the pistol and slid his finger onto the trigger.

"That's not black skin, it's a tattoo." Parlan pointed to Faison's hands. "Tattoos that move! How is that possible?"

"None of your business, wild man." Faison leveled the gun and fired.

Raimond saw the flash of the muzzle and the wobble of the gold ball. He twisted away, but the bullet caught the front of his shoulder and blasted through his back. His knees hit the floor with enough force to splinter joists and shatter nails, but he still warned the family off with his eyes.

"You're finished. Then I'll dispose of the rest." Faison's attention drifted to his leg. "This wound is healing. Those dogs aren't—"

Raimond bolted up and drove his fangs into the villain's skull, puncturing bone with the sound of popping champagne corks. He dodged Faison's windmilling arms and peeled half the skin off his face like a ripe peach. "Who targeted me for assassination?"

Parlan flinched at thundering from the floors below.

"I sealed the rest of the guards in the glass room with a spell." Kaleigh placed her palm on the quaking wall. "Not sure how long it will hold."

"Finish him, Raimond!" Parlan drew his dagger. "Or I will."

"Did you kill my parents?" Raimond's face grew black at Faison's nod. He slammed the man's bleeding head into the floor. "Tell me who ordered this!"

"Allemands." Faison choked on blood and bone. "Witches, just like the one you're in bed with."

"Allemands! We were right." Aveline scampered toward the fight. "His face is growing back!"

"Why?" Raimond grabbed Parlan's dagger and sliced Faison's shirt open, revealing the black scorpion inked over his heart. "Tell me why, and I'll kill you quickly instead of—what does this mean?"

"I searched the ends of the earth for ink and a magician strong enough to overcome—"

Raimond wrenched Faison's neck until his spine cracked. He began carving the tattoo out of his chest, moving slower with every shriek.

"You'll beg me for that secret—" Faison gurgled and vomited blood "—after you've suffered enough loss."

"I'll never beg you for anything. Why did you target me, you bastard? Why!"

"You were a threat, imbecile." Faison's body jolted with every whip of the scorpion's barbed tail under his skin. "Your parents didn't even know their lineage. You carry the blood of gladiators. Too trivial to make you special, simply enough to make you dangerous."

Raimond kept a vise grip on Faison's neck and looked back to Parlan in shock.

"Everyone sees your talent, except you." Parlan threw his arms out. "Even the enemy."

"The Allemands wanted you out of the picture, so they could take over France." Faison's legs gave out. "They paid me to end you. My choice to change you didn't sit well with them, but I couldn't let all that ancient power go to waste."

"Power for what?" Raimond carved around the scorpion's thrashing spikes.

"Raimond, stop!" Kaleigh held up her hands. "Don't cut that evil thing free!"

Faison's knees buckled. "To rule Paris, of course."

"I've lost my love for Paris." Raimond aimed the dagger directly at Faison's heart. "Years of your evil stole my home from me."

"Killing me will haunt you." Faison forced a smile. "Just think, we could be partners."

"Not in this lifetime, or any other." Raimond plunged the dagger deep and let Faison's body fall to the floor with the hissing scorpion still trapped inside his skin. The castle quaked beneath his feet.

"Those guards will break through any second, unless I reinforce the spell." Kaleigh sprinted for the stairs. "Raimond—the dagger. Don't leave it!"

Raimond threw his weight against the weapon in Faison's chest, expecting resistance. He wound up on the other side of a shattered bedroom wall, holding the Damascus steel blade in his hand.

"Magic, remember?" Parlan dragged his friend down an entire flight of stairs before Raimond regained his bearings.

Kaleigh met them at the landing. "I added a little to that containment spell, but those guys are strong."

"We need to get out." Anton spun around. "Where's Aveline now?"

Siras pointed down the long cross hall. Footsteps and pawprints glowed white against a layer of brown dust. "There."

"What are you doing, *mademoiselle*?" Raimond croaked. "Let's go!"

"Not without this." Aveline pointed to an enormous object covered in a perfectly pressed sheet. Perette tugged at the cloth with her teeth.

"We can't drag furniture out of here, dear." Raimond stumbled before righting himself.

Aveline yanked hard and white linen fell to the floor. "This is an artifact."

"The clock?" Kaleigh danced across the floor with her hands over her mouth. "*The* clock? I had no idea this was here…or anywhere, for that matter."

"Who cares about a moldy old clock?" Anton gestured toward the escalating noise. "We're not safe yet."

"Not just any old clock." Aveline ran her fingers across the polished wood and gilded celestial faces. "Look at the detail, the carved hands, the phases of the moon. This was a sacred heirloom of Queen Mary."

"Mary." Parlan took a few steps closer. "*The* Mary?"

"Mary Stuart?" Siras' jaw dropped at Kaleigh's nod. He flashed to touch the soft finish. "Dutch wood—"

"From a sailing ship." Anton whistled. "We shouldn't touch it."

Aveline stared at Raimond. "Both Mary and Francis believed this clock held tremendous power…something to do with the rhythm of time. It stood in their bedchamber at Palais de Louvre and traveled with them everywhere."

"Legend says that the bottom shelf held their wedding keepsakes." Kaleigh crouched. "Last I heard, this antique was at Chenonceau when the chateau was vandalized."

"Chenonceau, my favorite." Aveline grabbed Kaleigh's hand and squeezed. "Castle of the Ladies."

"Ransacked by—" Anton tapped his forehead.

Siras snapped his fingers. "Queen Catherine. Not a nice woman."

"Just a legend?" Raimond felt his way along the dark shelf. Before he reached the back, his hand landed on faceted glass.

"Depending on who you believe." Kaleigh leaned all her weight into the base of the clock and it didn't budge. "Everyone was afraid it had been destroyed."

"What is this?" Raimond uncorked the bottle and sniffed. "Whiskey?"

"Considering what happened to our Queen, and her husband who certainly did not defeat time," Parlan retreated, "it could be cursed poison."

"Finding this is a blessing." Kaleigh shot Aveline a smile. "For our families."

"Bourbon?" Raimond sniffed again and took a cautious sip. "Blood bourbon."

"It's booze, who cares?" Aveline crossed her arms. "I won't leave without the clock."

"Fine." Raimond jammed the odd-shaped bottle in his pocket and signaled to his companions. "Let's tip this relic on its back."

All four vampires staggered under the weight, readjusting it on their shoulders twice before beginning the slow procession down the final set of steps.

"This must be over a thousand pounds," Parlan groaned.

"Kaleigh, stop pushing me," Anton snapped. "What is wrong with you?"

"The guards are battering through the frame of that door." Kaleigh looked back and darted ahead. "I've got nothing to stop them."

"We can't put this monstrosity on a horse." Anton swayed and nearly dropped his end. "Please wave your wand and make it lighter."

"Careful, it's delicate." Aveline picked splinters off the marble floor and jammed them in her pockets. "How about the carriage we saw earlier?"

"Get the wagon, Kaleigh." Raimond growled. "Now. Move!"

By the time they lugged the clock through the front door, dawn threatened the distant skyline and Kaleigh had maneuvered the carriage across the gravel courtyard.

"We're cutting it close." Parlan heaved his end of the antique into the back of the wagon. "Hopefully these curtains offer some protection."

"Everybody in." Raimond grabbed Anton and Siras, boosted Aveline into the carriage and jumped in behind her.

The wolves burst out of the dark portal, dashed across a field of wildflowers and disappeared into the dense forest.

"Wait!" Aveline emptied the splinters from her pocket into the bottom shelf of the clock. She ran her hand across the hinged front door until her fingers found empty holes in the polished mahogany.

"The knob fell off. The artifact needs to be complete or it's worthless."

With the threat of dawn simmering behind the royal treetops, Aveline darted past Raimond. She slid through the castle door.

"Aveline, come back!" Raimond leapt from the draped carriage, jingling the missing hardware.

Sounds of cheering echoed from deep in the castle.

Raimond sprinted toward the castle door. "Aveline, run!"

A hand shot from the darkness and clamped around Aveline's throat. The attacker dangled her over the threshold by her neck.

Raimond dodged vicious rays of day that broke over the roofline. Smoldering black patches on his skin forced him to a stop. A shaft of pure sunlight blocked his progress, driving him back a step at a time. "Let her go!"

"You killed our sire. You deserve to die!" the tall guard screamed. "But this little trollop will do."

Kaleigh jumped from the driver's bench of the carriage and charged past Raimond. She jammed a handful of paper tubes in his hand and strode forward, spraying flames from her palms with each step. The guard dropped Aveline and ripped off his burning coat.

"Raimond!" Aveline dug her fingers into gravel and struggled to stand. "Perette!"

Raimond inspected the brightly colored parchment in his hand. "What—"

"Fireworks." Parlan flashed to Raimond's side and struck a match on the bottom of his shoe. "Flaming spears."

Raimond launched a sparkling stick at the guard and carved a chunk of flesh from his hip. The man was blown back, but immediately scrambled forward with his solid black eyes locked on Aveline.

Kaleigh reached Aveline at the same time the imprisoned guards stampeded into the grand hall. Her fire barely slowed them down. The first charging vampire threw her across the yard. Kaleigh's head struck the carriage wheel and her body landed like a pile of rags.

"No, no!" Siras flew to Kaleigh's side, prying her eyelids open. "Wake up witch-girl, we need your help. Where's Perette?"

The guards formed a boundary at the sunlight barrier. One dragged Aveline to the edge by her hair.

"Run, all of you!" Aveline howled as he forced her arm into the sun. "Take the clock and go."

"The hell with the clock." Raimond darted back and forth on the shadow line, searching for a way past the brutal sun. The jagged shade of the spires allowed him close to the castle, but never close enough. "Wolves!"

"Raimond Banitierre." A guard with glowing black hair and fiery blue eyes thundered across the courtyard. "You have committed treason. You, are responsible for killing Faison. You."

"Let Aveline go. She has nothing to do with it."

"You." The guards pointed and chanted as one. "You."

"Wait!" Raimond rushed into the sun and fell back as his skin blistered and flared. Deep in his skull, the echo of paws hitting grass grew louder by the second. "Please wait!"

"We will not rest until justice is served." The guards repeated the threat until every word blended into the ones before and after it, like a circular promise of doom.

"Set her free, and I'll give myself up." Raimond tumbled to his knees. "I beg you."

"You're finished, whether you surrender or not." To the applause of his friends, the blue-eyed vampire brandished a gold dagger in the air. "Shall I do it now, men?" The cheers grew louder and the guard pulled Aveline close and licked her cheek. "Or play with her first?"

Raimond's vision clouded with black and red spots. He fought off Parlan's attempts to drag him away.

The guard's gaze snapped to the castle gate. A silver shadow reflected in his blue irises. He plunged the dagger deep into Aveline's heart the second before Perette clamped onto his arm and severed it at the elbow.

The killer screamed at his shredded skin, kicked Aveline to the edge of sunlight and spit on her chest. "She's finished too. My bet is the sun cooks her before the gold."

"No, no, no!" Raimond crawled across the gravel. He reached for the shrinking girl, but the sun forced him even farther back. "I'll never abandon you."

"Run, Raimond." Aveline locked her eyes on his and managed a smile before her rosy lips waned to dusky grey. Her skin withered and clung to bone as the blotches grew darker and stole her face. "Follow the plan and disappear."

Parlan seized Raimond's shoulder. "We have to go!"

"I refuse to leave her." Raimond jerked free and clawed at his own eyes. "She's suffering."

The four remaining wolves converged on the guards, crushing them against stone walls and shredding flesh before chasing the vampires back into the castle. Perette lingered, nudging Aveline's arm and licking her ears.

Kaleigh staggered to her feet, dodged the chaos and slid to a stop next to Aveline's writhing body. She broke into sobs until Aveline clamped both palms onto her face. They shared a look and mumbled a short spell together. The air between them turned hazy and Aveline's arms collapsed.

"Can't you help her?" Raimond raked his fingers through his hair. "I never told her—"

"She's at peace now, Raimond." Kaleigh sprinted across the courtyard, grabbed his hands and forced them still. "Aveline loved you too, but we need to get as far away from this hell hole as possible."

Parlan hauled Raimond into the carriage by his neck. Cackling from above made them look up. Faison's wounded soldiers stood on the balcony above the door, cowering in the last moments of shadow.

"You." The blue-eyed guard leaned over the stone balustrade and shook the bloody stump of his mangled arm. "Enjoy your freedom, Banitierre, for it will not last."

"Wolves!" Kaleigh yelled from the driver's seat.

"They're coming." Parlan pounded on the side of the carriage. "Just go!"

Kaleigh slapped the reins and yelled. The horses trotted for a few seconds and then exploded into a gallop as they passed through an arch in the fortress' wall.

"One, two, three, four…" Raimond leaned out of the carriage and counted furry bodies as they darted out of the castle and crisscrossed behind the wagon. Massive gates began to swing shut. "Something's off…what's missing?"

The creak of rusty hinges made Raimond's heart scream as if it was being ripped apart. He stared into the broiling sunlight until he saw grey fluff cowering next to Aveline's corpse. "Perette—the gates! Run!"

The big wolves slid to a stop and whirled around in time to see a silver blur take aim at the vanishing sliver of escape. A last-second leap slammed her chest between the crushing iron bars.

"Don't give up!" Raimond's skull echoed with Perette's wails and the splintering of her ribs. "Fight! Do it for Aveline!"

The little wolf clawed and writhed her way up the barrier and squirmed through a tiny gap at the top. A motionless heap of fur crashed to the ground outside the gate.

Raimond leaned out of the carriage, cursed Chambord and screamed with all the strength he had left.

Perette staggered to her feet, pinned her ears back and launched away from the castle.

Chapter 11

EARLY WARNING

"DO WE NEED to act on our plan?" Parlan tried to engage Raimond in conversation each time Kaleigh slowed to determine their direction. "Because maybe not if—"

"Of course we do. I choose not to talk about it right now." Raimond stayed silent for the remainder of the day, filling pages of the angel book with memories of Aveline. When the wheels bounced in a pothole or slid in a rut, the jolts jogged loose more details along with things he never summoned the courage to say. He forced himself to stare past frayed curtains and tassels at the sunlight, averting his gaze only when the insides of his eyes boiled hard enough to burst, as if punishing himself for abandoning Aveline. But every time the pain subsided, guilt returned with a vengeance.

As the travelers put miles between themselves and Chambord, young thickets of native trees thinned into historic acres of oak mixed with mighty firs. At dusk, Kaleigh brought the carriage to a full stop under pines that soared and arched like nature's cathedral. She whipped the musty drapes back. "Sundown. These horses need a real break."

"Is she well enough to continue?" Raimond peeked past her at Perette's silver fur.

"She's nearly healed." Kaleigh stroked the wolf's neck. "Your blood was fresh in her veins."

"I felt every second of pain in her little heart." Raimond rubbed his chest. "Every ounce of grief for Aveline."

"Perette's bond to you will wear off in time." Kaleigh bit her lip. "Probably on the full moon."

Anton and Siras stretched, unharnessed all four horses and led them to the river. Parlan followed Raimond to the edge of the clearing, darted past and blocked his path. Every move Raimond made, Parlan anticipated.

"You're still determined that we separate?" Parlan stood his ground. "Why?"

Raimond hung his head. "Faison's men are hunting me, not any of you."

"I don't want to leave you alone, Brother." Parlan reached for Raimond's shoulder. "That was never the plan."

"But you must." Raimond pulled away to face remnants of the fading sunset. "I'll travel west. You will take the carriage and ride north to Paris, and then Le Havre."

"West?" Kaleigh walked up behind them, with wolves on her heels. "Looking for what?"

"The port of Brest." Raimond patted his pockets. "I'll book passage."

"Not alone, you won't," Parlan hissed.

"He won't be alone." Kaleigh pointed to the swirling wolves. "They'll travel with him. It's not safe for them to stay in France, either."

"He's going to run with wolves?" Parlan threw his hands in the air. "Someone explain how this is wise."

"Not run, Brother. Ride." Raimond's eyes fixed on a point beyond Parlan's back.

In fog at the fringe of the ancient forest, a grey stallion emerged like a phantom.

"Is that horse real?" Parlan asked.

"He followed us," Kaleigh said. "Brest is a hard two night's ride from here. I have enough incense left to cloak you for one."

"And the full moon." Raimond flipped his attention to the wolves.

"Two nights away."

"Plenty of time." Raimond clucked and the horse was at his side. Perette appeared at his feet. "Parlan, you'll take Kaleigh, and Kaleigh you'll take the clock."

Parlan screamed. "I still don't care about the bloody—"

"Aveline's final three words were about that bloody clock. She said, 'unlock the future'." Kaleigh rested her hands on her knees. "The spell is so complex, it may take years to break, but we can't just toss it on the side of the road."

"My darling Aveline." Raimond let his shoulders droop. "I failed her."

Perette whined and buried her face against Raimond's leg.

"Here's the truth." Kaleigh rested her hand on his chest. "Aveline was with child, but it was nestled outside the womb. If she remained human...no surgeon is skilled enough. Both would have perished. As a vampire, starving in Paris kept the child dormant. When she drank more blood, it grew larger and stronger. Her eternal life would have been...death was a blessing."

Raimond groaned and staggered away. "Buried in a curse."

Parlan chased Raimond back to the carriage with the grey horse one step behind. "I'll never rest with you wandering the globe."

Kaleigh cleared her throat. "I have one more gift for you, Raimond."

"The magic to make blood wine?"

"No, those instructions are already written and tucked into the front of each of your spelled books." Kaleigh pulled a silk handkerchief from her pocket and waved it over her head. "This was actually Aveline's idea."

A small flock of birds descended from the dark trees. Silver moonlight made the soft colors of their feathers glitter like the aura of a rainbow.

"Canaries?" Raimond held his hand up and let one land on his finger.

"Birds from the Blessed Isles." Kaleigh smiled as feathered orbs lit on her shoulders. "My flighty French employers brought them home from one of their exotic trips. As with most souvenirs, they grew tired of them and all the care fell to me."

"Do they drink blood?" Raimond asked.

"No silly, they eat fruit and seeds," Kaleigh said. "They'll keep you company, but more important, they'll be your alarm."

"In case cats show up to kill him?" Parlan ducked a diving bird. "He already has dogs."

"You're a funny one." Kaleigh caressed the air with her fingers as if she were a ballerina. Birds swarmed over her head. "They can sense dangerous magic, poison or holy fire...which, so you're aware, is a malicious lie masquerading as God's will."

"What about this beast?" Parlan picked reins off the mossy ground. The stallion eyed him, but quickly snapped his attention back to Raimond.

"I heard what Faison told you of your gladiator heritage," Kaleigh said.

"I guess that makes me the descendant of strong men." Raimond clucked and the stallion trotted to him with long graceful strides. "But also slaves, used just as Faison used all of us."

"There were a very few gladiators that earned Roman citizenship." Kaleigh pulled the tiny incense bag from her pocket. "I'd have to trace your specific lineage, but there's a good chance your ancestor was one of those warriors."

"You got all that from an obsessed horse?" Parlan asked. "With one green eye."

"Another trinket from holiday." Kaleigh rubbed the stallion's broad nose. "This one is from the mountains of Italy. The land of the free gladiators."

"You said Inverness, right Parlan?" Raimond swung into the saddle. "I promise, I'll get word to you."

"Travel safe, Brother."

"You too, Brother." Raimond nodded to Anton and Siras. "Men, take care of him."

Kaleigh lit the remaining incense and blew the smoke over Raimond and the wolves. Birds hovered in a vibrant halo around their heads.

"Be ready when I send for that clock." Raimond smiled and urged his mount into a gallop.

Two nights later in the coastal port of Brest, Raimond convinced the harbor master to write him six tickets for first class passage in exchange for a fancy saddle and bridle. Under a robust moon with sinister eyes, he boarded the galleon with four men and a honey-blonde woman, while a grey stallion paced the cliffs. After the ship's sails disappeared into the fog, the horse vanished in the direction of Paris.

Six weeks later, Raimond disembarked in Savannah, Georgia under a dead-calm and moonless sky. Five bony wolves swirled down the gangplank around him. Colorful birds hovered in the rigging before following them like glowing bullets.

PART II
EMILY

Chapter 12
WISE CHOICES

RAIMOND CHECKED TO make certain the docks were abandoned before signaling to the wolves with a low whistle, barely audible over the moaning of dock lines flexing in the tide. Five masses of fur materialized from behind rolled hay bales and bootleg liquor barrels. Perette's dull gaze wandered across the inlet to moss swaying from gnarled bayou branches.

"If you're feeling the call of freedom, I won't stop you." Raimond toed the warped dock boards. "But I believe I've found employment."

The wolves drifted closer.

"I've taken your worries about me working with sick humans very seriously but I knocked on the door of the local hospital, last night, at midnight. Never thought anyone would answer." Raimond shook his head. "A man did, an alarmingly young fellow. Once I convinced him I wasn't injured, he brewed coffee. We talked and finished the entire pot while he visited patients."

Five pairs of yellow eyes fixed on him at once.

"Sounds too good to be true, but he offered me a job as an orderly on the night shift. The position comes with lodging, as well, in an old building at the back of the hospital's property...near the garden and stables."

Five sets of ears perked up, one pair at a time.

"I've seen the place and it's run down, certainly, but built into a hillside with a cellar or cave of sorts. Plenty big enough to hide us all." Raimond pressed his palms together. "Shall we have a closer look?"

The parade of wolves, tiny birds and a vampire zipped across town, diving into the darkest gloom and avoiding every oil street lamp until they reached what was left of a formal park. The hospital dominated an entire side of the green. Directly across the square, vines aggressively devoured a sagging mansion. Beyond the once pristine veranda, overgrown flower beds crumbled into pulsating wilderness.

"Once upon a time, this was a grand home in a wealthy neighborhood." Raimond pointed out faint lights in a scattered few windows. "Apparently, the road continued another few miles, but one hellish storm reclaimed it as a swamp and people never rebuilt."

The wolves followed Raimond along the outskirts of the property, blending in and out of shadows thrown by misshapen trees. The last dash across an open field left their paws muddy.

"Hopefully that was the soggiest spot." Raimond flashed to a side door and ushered his friends in. "These front rooms aren't very usable. I'll make a show of fixing them up, but back here..."

The hidden portion was a maze of chambers sprinkled with old furniture and several exit tunnels. A safe place in a strange land.

"I promised to work a few hours tonight." Raimond quickly changed clothes and tried to ignore his companions' wide eyes and whining. His starched uniform shirt and matching white pants were the complete opposite of his normal attire. "I know, I look ridiculous. Carry on."

Time alternately dragged and sped by with Raimond reporting to work each night when the hands of the clock stood straight up and became one. His first assignment was scrubbing every surface in the hospital to glistening perfection, followed by a quick promotion to attending the needs of patients on the graveyard shift. The meager rotation of senior nurses and reluctant students welcomed his exceptional strength and endless energy, as if he was a savior from a mysterious land.

At three o'clock every morning, Raimond walked the perimeter of the property. The official reason was for security. His true motivation was a visit to the back house and a glass of blood wine to keep his hunger at bay.

As his hand fell on the doorknob, a dull thud and the clank of metal hitting stone disrupted the drone of marshland insects.

"Help!" a man croaked. "Is anyone awake?"

"Who's there?" Raimond followed the voice to the far side of a murky pond.

"It's me, Benjamin. I dropped my lamp."

"What are you doing out here at this forsaken hour?" Raimond found the sputtering lantern and turned up the flame. "And where are your crutches?"

"It was either a light or those damn sticks." Benjamin struggled to sit up and flailed toward an iron bench. "I nearly made it too. Can't an old man get a breath of fresh air without a catastrophe?"

Raimond wrapped his arms around Benjamin's waist and gently lifted him to the seat. "Does anything hurt?"

"Besides my pride, no. Well, maybe." Benjamin tapped on his left leg. "I cracked this ankle on a rock."

"Hold up the lamp. I'll take a look." He bent over and slid Benjamin's trouser cuff up. Blood erupted from the man's bony shin, painting Raimond's chest and face crimson. He clamped a shaky hand over the jagged gash. *No, no, not here.* The nighttime swamp orchestra faded into deafening silence as Raimond's chest ignited and his gums throbbed. Human blood dripped down his nose, into his mouth. *Not now.*

"Are you alright, son?" Benjamin lifted his lamp higher. "I didn't realize you were squeamish."

"I'm usually not." Raimond kept pressure on the laceration and turned away, burying the black skin of his face under his arm. Blood continued to pump through his fingers, drenching the grass and trickling down the walkway. The pit of his stomach twisted and ached. "You may have sliced an artery."

"Don't tell me I'm going to bleed to death next to an old goldfish puddle."

Raimond nicked his own wrist and rubbed black blood into Benjamin's leg. The wound's healing began in the deepest muscles that touched bone, sewing tissue and skin layers closed until nothing was left on the surface but a pink splotch. When he looked up, the old man's eyes were as wide as saucers. "Please, don't be frightened."

"I don't recall hitting my head." Benjamin leaned in with the lamp, examining the dark veins that traced an intricate map across Raimond's skin. "But I believe you just saved my life."

"You know I can't let you remember this." He locked his green tinged red eyes onto Benjamin's gaze. Inside his mind there were obstacles Raimond had never encountered before. Doors where there should have been windows. Brick walls where there should have been clear pathways. He stopped when Benjamin grabbed his head and moaned. "I'm sorry, it should be painless."

"I can barely remember what day of the week it is, so any recollection of tonight will be safe, lost and rattling around in the abyss." Benjamin patted Raimond's shoulder. "I'm not scared, just grateful. Remember son, everyone has their own demons."

Once a month, by the light of the full moon, Raimond took time off. His wolf companions were only human for a night and he relished those hours of company and conversation. The celebrations were feasts of fresh fruit, soft bread, aged wine and cuts of meat fit for kings and one queen. Every place setting was unique, complete and complemented by its own antique chair, salvaged from an abandoned neighborhood of magnificently decaying estates.

"This is truly delicious." The pack leader, Red, dabbed his unruly auburn beard with a linen napkin. "Can you not even taste a bit, Raimond?"

"No, well, not yet." Raimond savored the aroma of onions and seasoned beef spinning above the fire. "Though it brings back happy memories of my childhood."

"We've noticed that you can look out into the daylight almost without pain." Red pointed through a sparkling panel of glass.

"I've been conditioning my eyes for years, I guess." Raimond rubbed his chin. "Walking around after dawn, in the fog…that's a new skill."

"Varying your routine is wise. Keeps people from asking questions."

"As far as I know, nobody here suspects anything. Though there is one patient…a gentleman—"

"Too dangerous." Red ground his teeth. "Can't you erase whatever he saw?"

"His mind is much older than his years and painfully fragile." Raimond shook his head. "I couldn't take the chance of damaging it further."

"*Monsieur*, aren't you lonely?" The little silver wolf had become Perette for the night. "Have you not tried to make one of your own kind yet?"

"I know the process." Raimond pictured the page in his angel book and Aveline's handwritten instructions in invisible ink. "But I can't imagine inflicting this curse on anyone."

"You must miss home, though?" She twirled her blonde hair and brushed a crumb off the silk gown Raimond had given her as a gift.

"Paris, no." Raimond straightened the silverware alongside his pristine plate. "But rural France had a beauty I've not yet found in this country."

"We've traveled a bit." Red leaned back in his chair. "Beyond the swamp, fields of sugar cane rise to meet mountains crowded with forest. On the other side, sweeping plains and winding rivers stretch as far as the eye can see."

"I'll visit someday, when my work here is done."

"Which may be never." Perette stood and nudged lace curtains aside to peek through the window. "They're back."

On the path leading from the hospital to the buildings at the rear of the property, three figures appeared in the evening mist. An elderly man pushed one woman in a wheelchair, while another shuffled behind him with her cane.

"They're arguing." Red shook his head. "Again."

"I hear them." Raimond chuckled. "It's all a game. They'd be lost without each other."

While the pack cleared the meal off the table, Raimond threw the door open and stepped across the threshold. "Ladies and gentleman, do you require assistance?"

"We're almost there." The woman waved her cane. "Watch the rut, Benjamin, before you dump my sister in the dirt!"

"I've got it, Frieda," Benjamin grumbled. "Keep that stick on the ground or you'll be the one in a heap."

Raimond knelt to take the speckled hands of a woman slumped in her wheelchair. "Miss Lydia, how are you this evening?"

"Creaky and old." Lydia smiled. "But always delighted to see you."

"We know it's your night off, Raimond, but the staff...." Benjamin nodded back toward the main building. "They can't make the tea right."

"Ah, so this is all about the tea?" Raimond winked, lifted Lydia out of her chair and ducked inside the house.

"And the little birds." Lydia laughed into her hand. "I love to hear them sing."

Red arranged her wheelchair in the sitting room, but Lydia clutched onto Raimond's shoulders. "I'm afraid of the big dogs."

"Don't worry. I let them out back when I saw you folks on the path." Raimond glanced around at his friends trying not to laugh. "You're safe tonight."

Frieda shuffled through the door and stopped short.

Benjamin ran into her back. "What's the holdup? I nearly broke my nose."

"You should watch where you're going, old man." Frieda leaned back and whispered, "He has company."

Benjamin looked around the sitting room at five unfamiliar faces. "If we've interrupted…"

"No, no." Raimond ushered him to an armchair. "Dinner is finished."

"We were on our way out." Red nodded to his pack. "Perette, would you like to stay and help Raimond with the tea?"

She nodded and darted into the kitchen to boil water.

Raimond made Frieda comfortable on the old sofa before standing back and crossing his arms. "I've given the tea recipe to the nurses and all the doctors agreed that it was safe."

"I think…" Benjamin looked at his two friends. "*We* think, you make it better."

"It's the only thing that allows us to sleep at night and wake up without time's aches and pains." Frieda rubbed her knees. "You know my joints lock up."

"Clears out the clutter." Benjamin tapped his forehead.

Raimond took the steaming kettle and a jar of loose tea from Perette.

"There must be a secret ingredient." Lydia leaned forward.

"Hmm…" Raimond filled a sachet with leaves and flowers. "Ginger, cinnamon and a touch of bergamot."

The three guests rubbed their palms together as Raimond poured them each a cup. He saved the last of the boiling water for Perette.

"This is so delicious, Raimond." Frieda sipped and groaned. "Did you learn to make it as a child?"

"No, a young woman named Aveline taught me." A frown drifted across his face and he mouthed the word "sorry" to Perette.

"If I'd been…" Perette turned to the fireplace and dropped her voice to a whisper only Raimond could hear. "Just one second sooner, she'd still be here."

"Was Aveline your daughter?" Lydia asked. "Or wife?"

"I think you're prying, Lydia." Benjamin set his cup down.

"It's quite alright." Raimond looked out the window into the murky swamp. "Aveline was a nurse and a cherished friend. So many of the remedies I know, I learned from her."

"Did you love her?" Lydia asked.

Frieda patted Lydia's hand and held a finger to her lips. "Shhh."

"I believe I did," Raimond whispered. "But I never managed…"

"To tell her?" Lydia raised her eyes to meet Raimond's. "We ladies usually know."

"I sincerely hope you're right." Raimond read Perette's nod and smiled.

"Who hasn't made that mistake?" Benjamin struggled to stand. "Thinking we have time."

"We should get back." Frieda patted Benjamin's arm. "Before the staff finds out we've escaped."

"As if they didn't see us go." Lydia stretched out her shaky hand. One bright green bird landed on her finger and launched into song. "How I love these little darlings."

Raimond hooked his thumbs in his belt loops. "Would you like a pair, Miss Lydia? They would brighten up your room."

Lydia's eyes lit up. "If my sister says it's okay…"

Everyone in the room stared at Frieda, who threw her hands up. "How can I say no to that?"

"I'll build a cage and deliver them as soon as possible."

As the three visitors shuffled to the door, Lydia pulled on Raimond's sleeve. "It's ok to mourn your Aveline. But I'm sure she would want you to move on, to live your life in joy."

"You're absolutely right." Raimond secured Lydia's shawl around her shoulders. "But how will I know that I'm ready?"

"You'll just know, my dear." Lydia blew him a kiss as Benjamin rolled her chair down the bumpy path.

A few weeks later, the head physician offered Raimond a job as surgical assistant and apprentice. Later that morning, the clang of a metal breakfast platter against parquet woke him from a sound sleep.

He heard shouts from the far end of the orphan's wing and footsteps of day and night shift staff racing to investigate. He lurched to a window with the clearest view into the dining room.

Oh no, they're really going at it.

"What do you mean it changes nothing?" Frieda brandished her cane with enough force to make the newly hung chandelier jingle. "He's the only one who cares, and not just about the poor babies who live in this building."

"The man can't stay here forever." Benjamin shook his fist. "His dream is to be a doctor, you selfish old biddy."

"My sister's no such thing." Lydia careened through the door in her wheelchair and ricocheted off a wall. "We're all unwanted, but she's right. Mr. Raimond has cared for us like family."

"Watch where you're steering that thing, woman." Benjamin put his foot out to stop the runaway chair.

"How does he remember all of us?" Lydia set the brakes.

"He writes everything in that book," Benjamin said. "With the wings on the cover."

"The pages are blank," Frieda hissed.

Benjamin waved her off. "Maybe you need better glasses."

How do I get over there? Raimond snapped his fingers. *My old cloak!*

Raimond flashed through pouring rain and only slowed down after he ducked under the portico of the crisply painted dining wing. He discarded the soaked coat and stepped to the center of the tables. "Ladies and gentlemen, please."

"I apologize if I woke you with the ruckus." Frieda gestured to the steel tray. "You're a saint to us, Mr. Raimond."

"You know you're never a bother to me." Raimond took Frieda's hands. "Remember, I promised you and your sister a pair of song birds from the old world?"

"With all the work you've done fixing our place up..." Frieda hung her head. "You haven't changed your mind?"

"Absolutely not." Raimond crouched down to meet her eyes. "I've just finished building the cage."

Lydia clapped her hands. "The pretty, bright birds?"

"Those little treasures will be delivered to your room tonight."

"What's truly priceless is how you asked to hear our stories." Benjamin rubbed his fingers across the worn military medals around his neck. "You actually listen and recall our names."

"Every name." Frieda wiped a tear. "As if we elderly people still matter."

"Every voice matters. This promotion is a chance for me to try something new and fulfill my father's greatest dream." Raimond motioned to the dark halls for help. "And Benjamin, I will still listen to every story you tell, and commit all the details to memory."

Staff crept into the room and began putting the meal back in order.

"Allow me." The head nurse helped Raimond into his cloak. "You'll make a grand doctor, if you keep your hair properly trimmed."

He tucked his hair under the collar. "How do you know that's my plan, *Madame?*"

"I think everyone sees that fire in you, plus I fear war is on the horizon. We'll desperately need surgeons."

"Do you think I have enough…"

"Talent? You were born with it. Georgia's finest medical college is in Augusta, and my uncle is the director of admissions." She pulled a printed calling card from her apron. "You're going to break a few hearts when you leave."

"I'm extremely grateful, but we may be getting ahead of ourselves." He tucked the card into his breast pocket. "And that broken heart business is ridiculous."

"Sir, I respectfully disagree. Every single member of this staff will give you a recommendation." She took a few steps and paused. "Plenty of pretty ladies for you to court up in Augusta."

"I'm not ready."

"Someday, you will be." The head nurse smiled. "Choose wisely."

Chapter 13

LEGACIES OF THE FALLEN

THE DISMAL BATTLEFIELDS of the Civil War became the site of Raimond's medical residency. For a vampire, nourishment should have been plentiful, yet he rarely fed. The chaos was endless and the despair of war had turned the blood sour with agony and grief. Hunger was his relentless escort. Only writing the soldiers' stories in Aveline's book brought him peace, as if she still lived through pages blank to everyone but him.

So much death and misery. There must be something more.

"Moving this hospital was horrific." Raimond stood in the door of the infirmary tent and wiped fresh blood from his hands. Lined up under the dirty canvas, every bed was filled with soldiers who hovered between the worlds of the living and the dead. "We must be a hundred miles from civilization."

"There was no choice, Doctor." Nurse Sophie mopped sweat from her forehead and handed Raimond a towel. "General Sherman means to take Atlanta."

"As if the injuries from the mini-balls aren't gruesome enough." He tossed the stained towel aside and examined charts hanging off the foot of every cot. "These camp diseases are wiping out both armies."

Nurses shadowed him and transcribed every order he gave. "Tell us which to do first, Dr. Banitierre."

"I'm not even a doctor yet," Raimond mumbled.

Sophie scribbled notes on paper, doling out assignments to the ragtag team of young girls and old women who served as her makeshift staff. "You're the only one standing between these poor souls and a pine box." She nodded to the last bed. "That one's taken a turn for the worse."

Raimond flipped through the thick pile of papers on the man's clipboard. "How are you feeling, soldier?"

"Like I'm fixin' to die." The man coughed and spit brown sludge onto his shirt. "Didn't your dogs make the journey with us? I miss the little silver one sleeping at the foot of my bed."

"I had to send them away. This camp is much too dangerous." Beyond the canvas walls, a harmonica's bleak wail oozed into the night. *Without his wolves as lookouts, feeding would become so dangerous, starving was a grim possibility.* Raimond pictured Perette and her tears as he forced her to say goodbye. "What may I do for you, brave sir?"

"You've done all you can, my question is why? Why, spend so much time on…" The soldier dropped to a whisper. "A Union fighter in a Confederate hospital?"

"None of that matters to me or my colleagues. Not skin color." Raimond held his hand against the man's forehead and found him burning with fever. "Certainly not a flag or different uniform."

"I'm weaker with every passing hour. It will all be over soon." The man's voice cracked. "Am I wrong?"

"If only I could heal this. If I'd just found you sooner, before the infection spread to your blood." Raimond sat on the edge of the cot, checked the bandages and shook his head. "There is truly nothing—"

"If you can't, doctor." The soldier grimaced. "Then nobody can."

"Please, call me Raimond. Tell me what else you desire."

"That you call me Frederick and make my passing as painless as possible."

Raimond fought back the bitter taste that oozed from his throat. He reached into his pocket and sighed at the dwindling supply of brown morphine bottles. "That I can do."

"I need to write a final letter home, but…" He shifted the stump of his mangled right hand. "There's a few sheets of paper in my haversack."

"Consider it done." Raimond found a pen and an inkwell on the tiny bedside table. "I need to brush up on my English writing skills."

"You know I was a Union deserter, right?"

"You know I'm from France, *oui?*" Raimond smiled and produced a flask from his pocket. "Sounds like an interesting story."

"I was an original volunteer for President Lincoln, back in '61." Frederick laughed and motioned for the flask. "And, yes, the accent gave you away."

"Where shall I start?" Raimond held the pen ready.

"Dear Amy." Frederick spoke while Raimond printed. "By the time you read this, I'll be gone. I want you and the little ones to know I died with honor."

Raimond set down the pen, reached for the flask and took a deep swig. "You have children?"

"Two. Well, one daughter, who Amy swears looks just like me." Frederick rubbed the center of his chest. "We were expecting when I accepted Lincoln's offer of amnesty for deserters."

"I'm sure Amy didn't want you to re-enlist."

"A ghastly situation. She's originally from the South, but her family didn't own any slaves." Frederick took another gulp of liquor to stop his cough. "They moved back to Savannah after our wedding. I could have been murdering her father or her brothers."

"I spent many years working in Savannah." Raimond propped Frederick's shoulders up. "A beautiful city."

"Do you have children?"

Raimond forced himself to breathe. "No, not yet."

"Don't worry. You have plenty of time to find the right lady and start a family." Frederick winced. "I'm sure Amy will return home if this war ever ends. If there's any home left."

"And what else shall we tell Amy? How about a few adventures she can reveal to your wide-eyed children at night by the fireplace, so they can remember their heroic father?" The second page of the letter sketched out Frederick's last days.

Frederick exhaled after the final line. "So no one ever wonders what happened."

"You didn't have to mention me by name." Raimond guided Frederick's shaky signature. "I'm only doing my job."

"I've written to her about you before." Frederick's cough wracked his body. "Hopefully she could read my left-hand scrawl."

"How long have you known one another?"

"Since we were ten years old."

Raimond chuckled. "I'm sure she figured it out."

"You treat every soldier and caregiver here as if they're family." Frederick shook his head at the carnage and sorrow strewn about the tent. "Granting me peace and dignity at the end is priceless."

"Your loved ones will treasure these words." Raimond dated the letter October 11, 1864. He folded the paper and tucked it in the pocket of Frederick's uniform jacket.

"The time." Frederick wiped a stray tear from his cheek. "The waste."

"My brother Parlan said those exact words, many, many years ago." Raimond sighed. He signaled the nurse to bring him a syringe. "I promise that letter will be delivered. I'm honored to know your life and your incredible story."

"You'll write it in your little journal?"

"I will, and I'll keep it alive as long as I walk the earth." Raimond filled the syringe and tapped out an air bubble.

"Before you do that—" Frederick stopped the needle just short of his vein and fumbled in his pocket for a package.

"Cigarettes?" Raimond took the pouch and struck a match. "Would you like one?"

"Join me." Frederick wrapped his lips around the brown paper. "Make no mistake, these aren't plain cigarettes."

Raimond lit his own and pulled a deep breath. "They smell like incense."

"Cloves." Frederick leaned back and let the smoke numb his pain. "Calms my nerves and insulates me from the hellish noises in this camp."

Raimond took another drag and felt the pounding heartbeats of human suffering fade into the background. "Quite amazing."

"My parting gift to you." He pointed to the morphine. "I'll take that now."

Raimond injected twice the normal dose and grabbed Frederick's hand. "Close your eyes."

"I sense your heart is broken too, kind Doctor Raimond." He drew a ragged breath. "My time is over, but yours is just beginning. Live it well in tribute to those who have made the ultimate sacrifice."

Frederick's heart thudded its final, erratic beats. The soldier's soul stepped from his broken body as a handsome young man, complete, happy and free.

After covering the corpse with a sheet, Raimond wandered out the back of the tent. Rain from the latest cloudburst had turned the dirt path into a river of muck. Steam from the ground mixed with smoke from the distant flames, making the stench of death an inescapable fog. All Frederick's memories were crystal clear in his mind: his parents, his love story, his children and his gallantry.

This is my purpose, the gift Aveline spoke of...protecting the legacies of the fallen. Not sure why it took me so long to understand. Raimond kissed the cover of the angel book. *She said I could do great things and I will. Now, I'm finally ready to move on.*

Raimond concentrated on a horizon that should have been dark and serene. Tonight, it glowed red with mayhem and fires ignited by the Union army.

As soon as this bloody massacre ends.

Chapter 14

NO PEACE

IN THE FADING moments of twilight, Raimond slipped onto the railroad platform. He flipped up the collar of his long grey coat against an odd whip of cold wind in the South. *Sure doesn't feel like April.*

"All aboard for Augusta. Final call!"

Raimond patted the pocket that held his journal, glanced at his ticket and boarded the least crowded train car.

The conductor secured the doors behind him. "Anywhere you can find an empty seat, Lieutenant."

"I hold no rank, sir. I'm merely an assistant surgeon."

"I watched you carry fallen soldiers to boxcars as if they were sleeping children and cover them with flags." The conductor saluted him. "You should be awarded the highest rank."

"Those men are the ones who made the staggering sacrifice. We're blessed this conflict is finally over." Raimond tipped his hat and ducked into the nearest compartment.

A young woman snapped her tiny jeweled mirror shut and tucked a pot of beeswax in her pocket.

Raimond stopped in the doorway. "My apologies, *mademoiselle.*"

"No, please. My goodness you're..." She sprung up, her eyes flicking from his polished shoes, up the braid of his sleeve to the ribbons and crosses pinned on his chest. Her gaze zeroed in on his green eyes. "Quite tall."

Raimond introduced himself while he admired her porcelain skin and full lips. "I may have the wrong seat."

"Nonsense, I welcome the company. I've changed trains so many times between here and New York, yet I feel like I've been alone for days."

"New York City?" Raimond raised an eyebrow. "What's your final destination?"

"Augusta. There's an incredible shortage of nurses, even now that the war is over." She offered her hand. "I'm Emily."

Raimond's hand dwarfed hers as he peered past her long lashes to find dancing blue eyes. "What a coincidence. I attend the medical college in Augusta. Are you old enough to be traveling alone?"

"As far as anyone knows, I'm perfectly legal." Emily's laugh floated through the car like a soft melody. "So, you're a doctor?"

"Not yet, Miss Emily." Raimond unbuttoned his long coat and took the seat across from her. "Though I've mastered some surgical skills."

"On the battlefield? I'm sure you have."

"By necessity, but I still need to complete the formal portion of my education."

"Let me fix that." Emily pointed to a frayed button. "I've promised to work at the hospital affiliated with a medical school."

Raimond's stomach fluttered and he fought back a grin. "We may be colleagues."

"You don't say?" She pulled a sewing kit out of her satchel and waited while he peeled off his coat.

Raimond watched her skillfully repair the uniform. "Thank you."

Emily's eyes traveled from the pressed cuff of his shirt to the black hair arranged over his collar. "My pleasure."

"Since you're from New York," Raimond glanced out the window. "I'm sure you're up to date on current events. What have you heard of Savannah?"

"Mercifully, Savannah is safe. General Sherman didn't burn it."

"That's a relief. We heard the news in camp, but all sorts of misinformation and rumors made their way through as well."

Raimond closed his eyes and let his head fall back. "I have many friends there."

"Sherman gave the city to President Lincoln as a Christmas gift." Emily fished through her bag again. "I brought a few newspapers. I wasn't sure what would be available. Here's the latest one declaring peace."

Raimond eagerly accepted the papers and smiled at Emily, who twirled her blonde curls. "We could all use a little peace."

The conductor rapped on the compartment's window. "Folks, I have some bad news."

"So much for peace." Emily shivered.

"I'm sure it's just another schedule change." Raimond's eyes searched the conductor's pale face. "Or not?"

Emily leaned across the aisle, grasped Raimond's hand and began to shrink back. "I'm sorry, I—"

"Not at all." Raimond inhaled a wisp of heady jasmine and squeezed her hand in both of his without looking away from the conductor. "What has happened?"

"The President—" The conductor removed his cap and bowed his head. "President Lincoln has been assassinated."

Chapter 15

MIRACLE OR MISTAKE

RAIMOND SAT ON the roof of Augusta's hospital, the tallest building in the city. He gazed past blocks of homes twinkling with gas lamps, all the way to the bustling riverfront.

"Your coffee." Emily handed him a mug and flopped onto the bench next to him. "Sure you don't want cream?"

"We've worked together for months." Raimond glanced at strands of hair that escaped her nursing cap. "Do I ever take cream?"

"You do not." Emily waved him off with a grin. "Has it really been months?"

"Time flies. May I have one of those sugars from your pocket?"

"The details never escape you." Emily handed him a tiny paper package.

"You look tired, *mademoiselle*. Where's your coffee?"

"Well, it's three in the morning, and you know I prefer tea. I get assigned this shift a few times a month, but you work it by choice. And you're wide awake."

"What can I say?" Raimond sipped his coffee. "It's a gift."

"Forgive me, I'm exhausted." Emily pulled a deep breath and turned to face him. "But I've finally worked up the courage to ask you—"

"Help!" A senior nurse burst through the stairwell door, gasping for breath.

Emily slapped her forehead. "I don't believe it."

"Dr. Banitierre," the nurse screeched, "you're needed."

"Right here!" Raimond handed Emily the cup and rushed for the door. "Deep breaths, *madame*. Tell me where to go."

"I'm Sophie." She pointed to the nametag on her ample chest. "Remember?"

"Of course, Nurse Sophie." Raimond clasped his hands behind his back. "Where am I needed?"

"Emergency Ward." Sophie adjusted the lace of her unbuttoned collar. "Lady from Savannah—demanding to see you. Only you."

"Savannah?" Emily took a quick swig of the coffee before handing it to Sophie.

"Yes." She nodded down the stairs. "And you'd better follow that doctor of yours."

"What does that mean, 'that doctor of yours'?"

"Well, you two seem very close." Sophie sipped the coffee. Her face remained blank. "You usually help him with children."

"Oh my." Emily grabbed the cup, gulped, gagged and shoved it back. "Raimond...I mean Dr.—never mind. Little ones are not his specialty."

"He's quite capable of treating infants, Emily." Sophie tossed the empty cup aside.

"Don't you think I know—" Emily halted halfway through the door. "Did you say infant?"

Sophie smirked.

"Just mind your business, old crone." Emily chased footsteps down the winding staircase until she caught up with Raimond. "Who would come all the way here from Savannah?"

"I had patients there. More like extended family." Raimond hurried her through swinging doors. "They know I work here. I get letters every week."

"Aren't they elderly folks?"

"In their eighties by now." Raimond jogged down a long hall. "Something must be very wrong."

"Why in the middle of the night?" Emily scooted ahead of him, pulled a bleached curtain aside and stopped short. "Definitely not eighty."

A petite woman sat on the stretcher. A little girl's face was buried in her skirts and a loosely swaddled baby rested in her arms.

"Dr. Banitierre?" The woman's eyes searched the space behind Emily.

"Yes, what brings you here Ma'am?"

"I'm Amy, Doctor. It's my son."

Raimond jerked back and scrutinized the children and then their mother. "Amy? Frederick's wife?"

"Yes, yes!" Amy grabbed Raimond's hand. "My Frederick wrote to me about how you saved all those injured soldiers. He said, if anyone could heal a person, it was you."

"I couldn't save your husband." Raimond shook his head. "I promise you, I tried my best."

"Kind sir, you did save him. His soul is free." Amy touched her son's cheek. "The doctors in Savannah say nothing can be done but I don't believe them." A tiny limp arm fell out of the blanket. "Please, please, please…"

Raimond grabbed the baby from her arms with gentle hands and shrugged the blanket away. He dropped his ear to the little chest. "Heartbeat is very faint. Respirations are shallow."

"He's terribly grey." Emily found a stethoscope and placed the earpieces in Raimond's ears.

"His lungs sound wet." Raimond nudged the earpieces free. "Miss Amy, has he fallen in water?"

"No, oh dear God, no." Amy wrung her hands. "He had a high fever. It lasted days; I couldn't break it."

"Any rash?"

"No, Doctor."

"And your daughter?" Emily looked at the little girl.

"She never got sick." Amy brushed her daughter's hair off her face. "Praise the angels."

"Beautifully said." Emily squeezed Amy's arm and looked to Raimond.

"The boy's condition is grave." Raimond glanced around the Emergency Ward, aware of many eyes on his back. "Nurse Emily, can you direct the ladies to our waiting area so I can examine…"

"Freddie," Amy whispered as she walked away. "I couldn't name him anything else."

Raimond caught Emily's attention before she pulled the curtain. "Stand right there. Don't let anyone else in."

The baby barely whimpered as Raimond laid him on the stretcher. Making as much noise as possible, Raimond rattled bottles and instruments to disguise his search for a simple syringe. Without unbuttoning his sleeve, he aimed the needle at his own wrist and withdrew a vial of dark blood.

"Are you forcing him to drink water, Raimond?" Emily whispered through the curtain. "Don't you need my help?"

"In a minute." Raimond struggled to find a vein in the shriveled child. *This is worse than I thought.*

"What if he chokes?"

"He won't." A feeble spurt of blood was the only indication of success. *I've no idea how much is enough, or an overdose.* He injected half of what he normally used on an adult and slipped the syringe into a hidden pocket. *Not to mention, completely unethical.*

"Raimond, I can't hold them off anymore." Emily cleared her throat and slipped between the curtains. "Mother Superior is marching down the hall right now."

Raimond strode around the stretcher and whipped the drapes back as a parade of nuns filled the ward.

"Your cuff, Raimond. Blood," Emily hissed as she picked up the whimpering baby.

"Reverend Mother." Raimond tucked his hand behind his back and smiled. "Little Freddie's condition has improved."

Freddie coughed and his eyes flew open.

"I can see that." The nun peered at the infant just as he let out a deafening wail.

"Look at his color! He's pink and wide awake!" Amy rushed in and held her arms out. Freddie shook clenched fingers and bawled in his mother's ear. "And hungry...I just knew Dr. Banitierre could save him."

"Strong work, Doctor." Mother Superior nodded to him and scowled at Emily as she left the room. "Nurse."

Amy cooed to Freddie as he gulped a bottle of warm milk. "Take it slow little man."

"Excellent appetite." Raimond scribbled notes in a chart and reached over to feel the baby's forehead. "No fever."

"How did you know her husband?" Emily whispered from behind frosted glass doors as she restocked the cabinet.

"Frederick was one of my patients back in the battlefield hospital. His death was what convinced me."

"That you were meant to be a doctor?" Emily asked. "Because everyone, including me, has been assuring you forever."

"It's more complicated than that." Raimond held his finger to his lips. "Frederick's tragedy made me realize my life's true purpose."

"Whatever you did, write it in your book. The private one."

"Wait?" Raimond froze. "What?"

"Yes, I have quite a list of questions, specifically about that spot of blood on your sleeve." Emily flounced behind Raimond with an armful of supplies. "But, officially, I'm so proud to be your..."

"Friend?" Raimond tapped his pen on his chin. "My nurse?"

"Your lady."

Raimond shot a smile over his shoulder and turned back to the busy ward wearing a fake frown.

Chapter 16

DEGREES OF FAILURE

IF THE YEARS of gruesome war that had served as his residency were nothing like Raimond expected, the formal portion of his training was everything he had dreamed of. He finally admitted to himself that the Savannah head nurse's warning about pretty ladies had been correct. Until recently he managed to remain unattached, buried in official studies and his private obsession to replicate blood bourbon.

Raimond shuffled from the library, across the center hall of the medical college. Elegant shadows thrown by moonlight and columns rippled across his back as he descended stairs to the basement. Never looking up from his textbook, he sat down in front of the bulky microscope, stared through the eyepiece, sniffed an uncorked bottle beside him and scowled.

"Still having difficulty?" A musical voice drifted in from the corridor.

"What in the world?" Raimond shot up, rattling every piece of glass on the counter. "Emily, you should not sneak up on a man like that."

Emily moved through pools of gas light as she glided across the dimly lit lab, fading from view and reappearing like an exquisite ghost in lavender lace. "When else can you and I have an uninterrupted conversation, Doctor?"

"Not a doctor yet." Raimond rushed to the door and peered up and down the hall outside the lab. Once he was positive they were alone, he twisted the locked and snapped the blinds closed. "Not ever, if I don't graduate."

"Stop worrying, silly." Emily removed her jaunty ribbon-draped hat and plucked hair pins out of her piled curls, one at a time. She fluffed each blond tendril but kept her velvet gaze on his face. "You're the finest student at this college and at the top of your class."

"You know I'm not truly prepared for…" Raimond gazed at her hair, glimmering in the delicate light. He swallowed hard as she slipped closer. "Whatever is happening between us."

"Have I competition?" Emily batted her eyelashes.

"My dear." Raimond shook his head and smoothed the page he was reading before quietly closing the ledger. "It's not proper for you to be here at this hour. Alone."

"You're forgetting I'm from New York City. It's a little different there."

"Still, if the Sisters found out I was taking advantage of a young nurse, they would—"

"Do nothing. I'm not a member of their convent. I've taken no vows." Emily placed a hand on her hip and smirked. "Besides, we're in a lab, surrounded by beakers and body parts. I'll wager they won't tattle."

Raimond leaned on the steel counter and fought his urge to laugh. "You don't know my entire story."

"I know what matters. You treat the patients with dignity, like humans instead of numbers on…" Emily reached out and shoved a pile of papers across the table.

"Every doctor does that." Raimond slumped back onto his stool. "Or they should."

Emily wiggled one finger. "Most do not. Unless the patient has money or influence, they're treated like medical experiments. Expendable."

Raimond swiveled to face the darkest corner. "That is one thing that I will change, whether I graduate as a doctor or not."

"Why in the world do you not believe in yourself?" Emily rested a hand on his shoulder.

"Sometimes, it still feels like I'm living a fantasy I don't deserve. There must be gossip about how I got accepted to study at such a prestigious college." Raimond rubbed his forehead, stood and paced the floor. "I offered no previous experience, no formal transcripts."

"You're a battlefield surgeon."

"I felt like the grim reaper, mangling people." Raimond shook his head. "Horrific beyond words."

"The essence of any talk I've heard sounds more like legend." Emily came up behind him and slid her arms around his waist. "At your Savannah hospital, you worked every night shift for years before applying to this school?"

"I took one night off every month."

"Well, apparently you impressed the doctors in charge. Surely made waves with the nursing staff." Emily closed her eyes and rested her cheek against his back. "And not just the charming, young ones."

"I focused on working with each senior physician. Assisted in all manners of surgery, accompanied them on every emergent house call." Raimond raked his hand through his hair. "Anything and everything they asked."

"As if you knew what those doctors needed before they did." Emily released him, turned and propped her elbows on the counter. "Were you really a soldier in the French army?"

"A commander, in fact."

"That doesn't surprise me, except…" Emily tapped her cheek with her finger. "Shouldn't you be more bossy?"

Raimond rounded the corner of the lab counter and stopped in front of Emily. She stepped forward. He slid back.

"That's what I mean…the hesitation." Emily closed the distance between them until he backed into a wall, with no more space to retreat. She ran her fingers along the lapel of his white coat, flicking off invisible dust before looking into his eyes. "Remember the evening we met?"

A smile tugged at the corner of Raimond's mouth. "How could I forget?"

"I'd love to see you in your uniform again. Or out of it."

"I'm not sure this is wise." Raimond placed a finger under her chin. The soft light made her glow like a goddess.

"Wisdom is overrated. Passion rules the world," Emily whispered, skimming her hand over his neck. She toyed with the long hair that rested on his collar, wrapping a strand around her finger. "Didn't you just visit the barber?"

"Yes, but it's raining."

Emily's slow nod eroded into a wobbly shake.

Raimond wrapped his hand around her waist, started to push her away but pulled her body close instead. "See, there are still things you don't know."

"Show me." Emily stood on her toes to reach his lips.

Raimond swept her into an embrace and her feet left the floor. He pressed his lips to hers, devouring her, crushing her body as he kissed her again and again, savoring the scent of rich jasmine floating in the air.

She trembled as a soft moan escaped her throat, but instead of shrinking back, her kiss searched deeper.

Raimond spun her around and thrust her on the counter, scattering bottles and corks like marbles.

"What is all this jumble?" Emily smiled and waved a faceted bottle under her dainty nose. "Smells sinful."

"That is still in the research phase." Raimond plucked it from her hand. "An ancient recipe that I'm trying and failing to replicate."

Her finger traced the line of her collar, drifting downward and pausing over her breast. "When it's finished may I taste it?"

"Possibly." Raimond grasped her face with both his palms. "Sweet lady, there is so much I've not told you."

"I've read books, Raimond. Nurses talk."

"Not about the act, *mademoiselle*." Raimond fought the urge to claim her body. "You may run when you learn the whole truth of my history."

"I'll take the risk." Emily looked at his lips and then straight into his eyes. "Less talking, more kissing."

Chapter 17

A GLIMPSE OF THE MONSTER

SEVEN STRAIGHT DAYS of rain, two tornados and one collapsed wall. After months of painstaking renovation, the little house still wasn't complete, but tonight's dinner had been set for weeks—and Raimond couldn't put Emily off any longer. He paced back and forth across the patio, adjusting tables and fluffing pillows.

What a mess. I'm a doctor, not a decorator.

All the original furniture had been moved out of his living room during construction.

These antiques might save the night. They ooze elegance, like the parlors of old Paris.

When the cottage was on the market, he had no trouble entering, as if it were free territory. Now, a wistful look through the dark windows was the closest he'd come to seeing the project since the house had secretly become Emily's property.

I need to figure out a way for her to invite me into a house she thinks I own.

Raimond struck a match, ignited a taper and went to work coaxing a sea of candles to life.

Emily will love the ambiance. Unless, of course, this whole date is a colossal mistake.

Raimond first lit hurricane lamps hanging from the trellis.

What if I hurt her?

He hadn't lain with a woman since his days as a Commander.

This will be Emily's first time. Mine too in a way, since on the last occasion, I was still human.

He moved on to candles in mismatched urns along the walkway.

We could just drink wine and I'd keep my promise to explain everything.

He blew out the taper and grunted at the tangle of curtains.

Supposed to be a luxury tent. Resembles the dressmaker's remnant section…or a whorehouse.

He wrestled to tie back fabric he'd draped across the low wooden structure.

Emily. Raimond pounded both fists into his forehead. *Emily.*

Scores of tiny flames cast dancing prisms of color through the lush garden hideaway.

It's been years. If I keep dragging my feet, I might lose her. His mind wandered back to the head nurse in Savannah and her counsel to choose his ladies well. *Emily did kiss me first. An angel with a touch of the devil.*

Raimond stood back and admired his handiwork. The delicate fragrance of night blossoms cruised on a breeze that toyed with hidden wind chimes. The setting whispered romance from the flower beds, but shouted seduction from the rooftop.

She's special.

He slouched onto an oversize chaise and rested his head in his hands.

But she's innocent. And I'm a monster.

Black veins exploded down his neck like ribbons of fire.

What if I can't control myself?

Heavy hoofbeats pounded the gravel road outside, growing louder and slower until they drew to a stop in front of the cottage. The creak of carriage doors was followed by muffled voices. One floated on the air like a feather.

"Raimond?"

"Back here, Emily." Raimond slammed the demon away and flashed under the portico. He threw his arms out. "*Bienvenue!*"

"You look so different away from the hospital." Emily planted a kiss on each cheek. She stood back and smiled at his unbuttoned charcoal vest and black shirt with rolled up sleeves. "So dangerous."

"You must have raided the brandy stash in my carriage." Raimond returned the greeting and brushed back green fronds of the side yard. "This is my casual attire."

"Wait—there's a stash? Never mind, I'm dying to see your new house." She peered under the low-slung porch draped with purple blooms. "Those vines look like they're dragging everything down."

"Yes, well, sadly the repairs are a bit more complicated than I expected."

"I love the twin chimneys."

"They're a unique element." Raimond pointed to the front door. "You may take a step inside. A cautious one."

"Oh dear." A gentle nudge swung the door open. She lifted her skirts and crept over the threshold. "Quite the disarray. Come, Raimond." She held out her hand. "Show me your vision."

"It's supposed to be a surprise, you know?" Raimond smiled with relief as he glided through the door frame. He found the architect's drawings on the stairs, unrolled them in the fading light and explained what still needed to be done.

"Will the kitchen be part of the main house?"

"Of course, but it needs expansion." Raimond pointed around the fireplace. "In the back, overlooking the garden."

"I can't wait to see it finished." Emily slipped back to the porch, plucked a flower from a wilting vine and rolled it in her fingers. "You won't tear these down, I hope?"

"I'll have my craftsmen prop them up." Raimond placed his hand on the small of her back. "Come darling, your celebration awaits."

"What's the occasion? Not my birthday." Emily tiptoed along the slate footpath and stopped short. She knelt and threaded her fingers through long grass. "So soft." Her shoes were off in seconds and she was ankle deep in green. "So cool. Feels like heaven."

Raimond followed her example and twirled her in a pirouette on the dark lawn. Two barefoot dancers in sparkling moonlight.

"You might be the most romantic man I've ever met." Emily tucked her head under his chin and swayed to imaginary music.

Raimond nodded toward the backyard and whispered in her ear. "There's more to see."

Ahead, a whitewashed garden shed gleamed in the clearing's corner. Framework over the door was draped with pastel colored linens and gauze. Lamps flickered in the rafters and candles painted designs on the patio.

Emily's jaw dropped as she crawled onto a huge sofa and sunk into the cloud of pillows. "You did all this?"

"To honor your job promotion." He uncorked a wine bottle and poured. "And new apartment."

"I was already scheduling the surgeries, you know? Only now, I have to order the supplies. It's soooo…not complicated."

"Still, all that work with no raise in pay." Raimond sat down, balancing the glasses. "But you're a master negotiator."

"Life in that convent was crushing me. Crushing us." Emily accepted the glass with both hands. "Don't want to spill."

"Won't matter." Raimond picked up a tasseled pillow. "My upholstery is the same color as your wine."

"The furnishings in my new home are sparse." Emily caressed the plush cushions. "Drab is a better word."

"What if that apartment was your official residence?" Raimond slid closer and pointed to the dark bungalow behind him. "And this was your true home? With me."

"That's positively scandalous." Emily sipped and grinned. "I did convince the nuns to allow me to move out, but they have spies all over town. Like my creepy landlord."

"Forget him." Raimond nudged the glass closer to her lips. "He'll be convinced you sleep in your own bed every night."

Emily closed her eyes and drained the glass. "I've not yet slept in yours, Raimond."

"Lack of privacy was an obstacle. But that's all changed." He took the empty glass and set it on a low table. Slipping his hands around her waist, he eased her onto his lap. "You're afraid?"

"Not at all."

"You're trembling."

"Okay, maybe." Emily tipped her hand side to side. "I know I've been pushing for this next step, but I feel a bit like a hypocrite."

"Because it isn't proper?"

"That's not...hardly. You know me better by now."

"If you aren't ready, just say the word. Your place is here with me and since I've graduated—"

"About that." Emily leaned in and brushed butterfly kisses from one side of his mouth to the other. "We should be—" She let out a long, low breath. "Celebrating you."

"I meant, as a legitimate doctor, I have a bit more stature to go with my long coat." Raimond locked his lips onto hers and pulled back to meet her eyes. "We could make it legal."

"Tonight?" Emily popped open one of his shirt buttons. "Right now?"

"It's a bit late for a man of the cloth. How about a judge?"

"Not necessary." Emily rolled her eyes and undid two more buttons.

"Or a ship's captain?"

"In Augusta?" Her fingers trailed up his sculpted chest and rested under his chin.

"From a riverboat?"

"The last thing we need is some salty sailor in our bed." Emily pulled one pin from her hair and sent waves cascading around her face. "What does a piece of paper prove anyway?"

Raimond's knuckles skimmed her cheek. "That I love you, Emily Gastrell."

Emily melted into his burning eyes. "Those words are proof enough for me."

"I never thought I would..." Raimond locked onto her gaze. "My heart belongs to you, *mademoiselle*."

"And mine to you, *monsieur*. How does one say 'I love you' in French?"

"*Je t'aime.*"

"*Zhe temm*, Raimond Banitierre."

"Perfect."

"No judgy riverboat priest needs to grant us permission." Emily sat back and bit her lip. "I know you're a man of the world. If I disappoint you—"

"Beautiful lady, that's impossible."

"To be clear, I'm not saying no. I just don't want your proposal to be rushed."

"I'll make it perfect."

"Unexpected and magical?"

"A spectacular surprise." Raimond pulled the ribbon on her collar.

"Such a tease." The neckline of her blouse loosened with each deep breath.

Raimond twirled the ribbon to the three-beat tempo of a silent waltz. "And I've not been a man of that world you spoke of in a very, very long time."

"I've taken your advice." She reached back to search for laces. "And started wearing this silly thing looser."

"So your lungs aren't crushed." Raimond chuckled. "Medicine trumps fashion."

"Still, I'm always ready to have this corset off."

"Why wear one at all?" Raimond removed his own vest and flung it away.

"Ooo, the gossip." Emily tossed the garment over her shoulder. "The outrage." She fumbled with her skirts while Raimond slid behind her and groaned at the caress of his fingers on her bare arms.

"Breathe. Listen to the birds sing."

"Those pretty, colorful ones?" She looked up. "They make the trees glow."

Raimond watched her shoulders relax as the bird's melody bathed her in tranquility. Emerald and silver fabric fell to her feet in waves, leaving her in a knee length chemise of pure white lace. "Only one petticoat?" A single move swept her into his arms. "Now, that's shameful."

Slow steps brought them to the edge of the cushions. Raimond raised his lips and brushed them lightly across hers. Emily winked and dove into his mouth with a searching kiss. They wound up tangled on the sofa in each other's arms.

"Is there nothing under this?" He pulled the loose chemise off her shoulder.

"The heat, remember?" Emily slid back, began lifting the thin cotton over her head and stopped. "Does this very charming tent close at all?" She pointed at curtains hanging around the trellis. "Or do the neighbors get a free show?"

"The neighbors are a mile away, but I planned ahead."

Raimond forced himself to walk and not flash to the drawstrings. Heavy fabric tumbled free, turning the extravagant setting into a private love nest. *Control, control, control.* With the long curtains closed and fluttering in the late-night breeze, he drank straight from the wine bottle and slid out of his shirt.

"Come here." Emily knelt on the sofa and motioned with her fingers. "Undressing you is my job."

Raimond watched her pull a long drink of wine and wiggle out of her chemise. His chest trembled where his heart had pounded long ago.

Emily pulled him close, until the bare skin of her breasts brushed his chest. She gently slipped a hand free and her fingertips wandered to his belt buckle.

Raimond's muscles quivered and a breath caught in his throat.

In one motion, Emily unclasped the metal and loosened the laces of his trousers until they drooped on his hips. She undid a singular button and inched the silk lower. Her eyes flicked below the deep V-shape of his waist and slowly climbed to meet his gaze.

"It's okay to look." Raimond swept a finger through her curls.

"Most girls do this in the dark the first time."

Raimond puffed out the brightest flame over their heads. He lingered while Emily's eyes burned a tantalizing path across his back. He returned to find her lying on her side, hugging a pillow. His fingers traced the back of her arm to the flare of her hips. "We'll take everything slow."

Emily discarded the pillow and pressed her soft curves against the length of his body. "Your skin is always so cool."

"I guess the heat doesn't affect me." Raimond shifted underneath her and skimmed the full length of her spine. "Maybe it's my French blood."

Emily's gasp was sweet melody in Raimond's ears as he cupped one breast in his hand and trailed kisses down the center of her belly. Her skin rippled as he drew circles behind her knees. "I promise not to hurt you."

"I trust you."

Raimond groaned and shivered as Emily's delicate fingers drifted below his waist. He slipped a hand behind her head and lifted a tangle of curls. "Why are you still so tense?"

"I know it'll be better for me the next time." Emily bit her lip. "I told you, nurses talk. They say the first time is always awful, but it makes the man happy. Eventually, I'll enjoy it too."

"Okay, hold everything." Raimond stood and unraveled a long piece of satin from the trellis. "Stand up. I won't peek."

"What in the world?" Emily giggled as Raimond wrapped the long train of fabric around her shoulders and spun her until she was draped in pink.

"Now." He sat down and pulled her onto his lap. "Be still in my arms."

"My dream is to make you happy, Raimond."

"You make me happy sitting on that swing in the hospital's courtyard."

"Pretend you're in that swing." Raimond rested his hand on her neck. "The birds are singing." He kissed her cheek, her nose and her other cheek. "Every flower in Augusta is blooming, and the scent reaches your pretty nose, one petal at a time."

"More than anything else, I want to be close to you." Emily shut her eyes and exhaled. She let Raimond lift her hand in the air and pressed her soft palm against his.

He alternated the pressure of each fingertip and smiled as she mirrored his rhythm. The back of his knuckles trailed up her arm, swirling inside her elbow and wandering across her flawless skin.

Emily explored his muscled arms and slipped her arm around the curves of his shoulders.

He loosened the end of the pink wrap and lowered her into a mountain of pillows.

This time, when Emily's fingers landed below his waist, she closed her eyes and pushed the silk shorts over his hips.

Raimond slid free of his last piece of clothing and kissed Emily's neck, inhaling the sweet scent of her flesh. His lips drifted under her breasts and around the sweep of her hips. She moaned as he kept going, until she was gasping for breath with shredded pink satin in her fists.

Emily twined her fingers into Raimond's hair and pulled him up until he was hovering over her. "I had no idea it could feel so…"

Raimond coaxed her knee to the side and rested his hips against hers. "Just one second of pain."

Emily's nails dug into his back and muffled her cry against his chest.

"Still with me?"

"Forever." Her body matched his slow pace and sped up on pure instinct, to meet his energy.

Softly. Raimond forced himself to concentrate on small movements. *Gently.* As Emily quaked and melded into his flesh for the second time that night, he relaxed and let go.

"Raimond!" She saw his face at the same moment he saw the gash in her neck. "What did I do wrong?"

"Damn it!" Raimond clamped a hand over his mouth, hiding razor-sharp fangs.

"Your eyes…" Emily clawed at his arms. "Skin—black!"

"Sleep!" He grabbed her chin and dominated her gaze. "Sleep, until I wake you."

Raimond waited for Emily's eyelids to fall, then lunged to put pressure on her neck and the two holes spurting blood from under her ear. He bit into his own wrist and rubbed black blood on her wound.

Emily's breathing faltered and her pulse skipped a beat.

"Em, stay with me!" He ripped his arm open again and forced blood down her throat. *Mais delivré-nous du mal.* With her face pressed against his chest, Raimond kept praying. *Or deliver her from evil at least.*

Emily drew a deep, human breath and let her hand drift over newly healed skin.

He raised his eyes to the sky. *Thank you, thank you.*

Her eyelashes fluttered but stayed closed while a smile and frown battled across her lips. She sighed as Raimond laid her back.

Raimond grabbed his pants and staggered toward the garden shed. He hurled a blood-stained pillow over the cottage's roof and searched for towels to erase any splatters of evidence. Party lights around the edge of the patio flickered and barely clung to life until he ripped a few ruined inches from the pink gauze and tossed it into one of the sputtering candles. The rest of the fabric was tucked around Emily's limp body while the miniature blaze illuminated her peaceful face.

I ruined your fantasy, sweet girl.

Raimond picked up her delicate wrist and felt a strong pulse.

My monster's blood is in your veins.

He swept damp blonde locks away from her face. The lump in his throat felt like a boulder.

And now, I need to make you forget things from a night that you should remember forever.

Minutes ticked by while Raimond wrestled with excruciating decisions.

Who the hell was I praying to? I'm losing my mind.

He lifted her as if she were fine china until she was cradled in his lap. "Wake up, Em."

Her eyes flew open. She recoiled with a shriek that slashed the heavy night air.

"Shhh, shhh." Raimond grabbed both sides of her head and forced her to focus on him. "I'm sorry." He loosened his grip. "I'm sorry I hurt you."

Emily stared through the hazy air, her lips forming silent protests.

"I'll explain it all, I promise. But, for now, I need you to forget what you saw."

"No." Emily's head shake became a reluctant nod. "But…"

"We made love. It was beautiful, right?"

"Amazing." Emily smiled and tried to break his lock on her eyes. "Raimond, please."

"Forget the blood, my face turning dark…forget my fangs. You were never scared." He swallowed hard. "*Oui?*"

"It was a lovely night." Emily's face melted into a pure smile. "Now I'm yours."

"And you're mine." Raimond released her mind.

Emily flopped on her back and let the late summer breeze cool her skin. "Fireflies."

"What's that, dear?" Raimond nestled her in the crook of his arm.

"I didn't see them before. But look, now they're everywhere, twinkling brighter than the stars. Like they're cheering for us." Emily caressed the strong line of his jaw. "*Je t'aime.*"

"I'm amazed by you. *Mon amour.*" Raimond laced his fingers into hers, kissed her hand and wrestled with the nagging voice in his head. *An angel in bed with a demon.*

Chapter 18

SPIES IN THE GARDEN

A QUAINT COTTAGE on the edge of town glistened in crisp October evening light. To passers-by it appeared as if no one was home, but below ground the primary resident was impatiently waiting for the sun to retreat.

Secrets don't last forever.

Raimond wrote in his journal, slammed it shut and opened it again to finish one sentence. He tossed it aside and drummed his fingers on the wall of a lead-lined, camouflaged room. His grand scheme no longer included living in rural Georgia.

Should have thought of that before I renovated this whole house.

The compartment he slept in was built by a singular craftsman, as a safe for valuables. If the worker had any questions about the large footprint and what would be stored there, he never asked, and his memory had long since been expunged.

Behind a sliding panel, the stockpile of blood wine was accumulating dust. Raimond hadn't bothered to fortify it in months. Aside from a simple cot and nightstand made of a packing crate, the only objects inside the room were his diary, experimental bottles of blood bourbon and one crimson pillow. The gold tassels and velvet reminded him of Aveline's wisdom and the Paris he adored in his former life. Back then, as much as he longed for family, he never dared dream of romance and a wife. Both seemed impossibly out of reach.

A safe home isn't a city or specific house, it's whatever space you share with loved ones.

Raimond's new plans sent him and Emily far enough away that they could marry and start fresh. Escaping without being discovered living in sin was essential. He crept upstairs a full hour before sunset, clenched his teeth and thrust his hand out of the dark safety of the hidden room.

No blisters.

He stepped into the heavily draped kitchen and lit the oven's coal fire before pulling a whole turkey from the icebox.

Probably not the best night to try out this new-fangled oven.

His freshly washed hands made the ink run on the instruction pamphlet's pages.

Damn it.

He jumped at a knock on the front door.

"Be right there!" Raimond grabbed a towel. The knock was louder the second time. "Hold your horses!" He flung the door open.

Two men on the porch took shaky steps back. "Apologies, sir, if we're too early."

"No worries." Raimond looked past them. "Did you bring it?"

The man on the left stepped aside to reveal a polished cherry dressing table.

"Splendid. And the mirror I chose?"

The man on the right held up a box. "Where should we assemble it?"

"Upstairs. Against the wall to the right of the bed." Raimond admired the scrolled antique as it was carried by, until the smell of cooking food reached his nose. "My dinner!" He dashed into the kitchen and opened the oven door. "I should take this thing outside and cook it over a pit. Too much coal on that fire." He waved a towel in the air to dissipate smoke and steam. "Don't I sound like an old man?"

"Doctor?" The delivery man poked his head through the kitchen door. "Are you speaking to someone?"

"Only myself, I guess." Raimond shrugged. *Like a crazy fool.*

"We've finished with the dressing table."

"And all the hardware is secure?"

"Yes, sir."

Tip money. Raimond patted all his pockets. *Empty.* He fished two bills and a handful of change out of his coat on the rack. "Much appreciated."

As soon as the delivery men left, Raimond pulled vegetables from a metal drawer and found a sharp knife. He julienned one carrot before a loud rap on the door interrupted him. Raimond craned his neck to see the wall clock. "Too early for Emily. I'll bet those fellas forgot a knob."

A voice boomed from the porch before the door was completely open. "Dr. Banitierre?"

"Yes?"

"Your message." A man dressed in head-to-toe black bowed and marched down the stairs to his horse.

"Thank you." Raimond popped the envelope's seal and shook his head. "So jovial."

Emily will be late, but she's bringing fresh bread. Good news, since the rest of her dinner is a bit haphazard.

After chopping a variety of vegetables, he added wine and spices to a clay pot and slipped it in the oven next to the turkey. He strode to the middle of the living room and took a long, cleansing breath. Above him, freshly sanded moldings gleamed with dark stain while reworked river rock framed the elegant fireplace. The craftsman had only finished a few nights ago, but their work was spectacular. Raimond checked the vegetables with a toothpick, fussed over the onion soup and drifted back to the living room in search of matches. From the built-in compartment on the mantle, he removed a set of silver tapered candles and his fingers grazed a trinket one of the workers unearthed during construction.

Only a truly honest man returns something like this.

Raimond flipped the velvet lid open and rays of emerald leapt out as if the box had barely held them in.

Footsteps on the porch preceded a light knock.

I hope the messenger doesn't want a tip now.

Raimond set the ring on an end table and opened the door while his mind rolled through excuses.

"Good evening, Dr. Banitierre." A stout woman dipped into a quick curtsy on the front porch.

"Bonjour, madame."

"You do speak French. Just like the neighborhood ladies said." The woman tucked flyaway grey hairs into her bun and tried to hide a giddy grin behind her sleeve. "Where are my manners? I'm Mrs. Crystal, from around the bend."

"Please come in, Mrs. Crystal." Raimond looked behind her and shook his head. He turned back, armed with his most charming smile. "Are the ladies with you?"

"No, no. I'm the welcoming committee for tonight. I've brought pecan pie."

"Thank you. Smells delicious." Raimond took the wrapped dish and nodded for her to follow him to the kitchen. "I'm cooking dinner now, or trying to."

"My goodness, I've seen this stove in the newest catalogs." Mrs. Crystal patted the middle of her chest. "My husband is a builder, you see, and I do have a modern kitchen but...I'm quite jealous."

"I've recently completed a renovation of the cottage."

"Yes, it's the talk of the town." She ran her finger across the oven's chrome handle. "This cobalt is stunning. Your wife is an excellent judge of color."

Raimond rubbed the back of his neck. "Miss Emily isn't...I mean, just not yet—"

"Lady friend, then?" Mrs. Crystal winked. "Ah, your sweetheart, and a proper lady. I've seen the carriage leave to take her back to town by eleven o'clock, every night."

"Um, may I ask your expert opinion? I'm confident about the soup, but everything else?" Raimond pointed to the smudged instruction manual and grabbed two pot holders. "Am I headed in the right direction?"

Mrs. Crystal admired the stewing pot of vegetables Raimond placed on the stovetop. He rummaged through two drawers before he found the silverware and handed her a fork.

"Carrots are very tender." She blew on the squash before tasting it. "And these are finished. Into the warming chamber right away, before they get soggy."

"The bird?" Raimond slid the pan out. His winced the instant heat hit his eyes.

"Careful, stand back when you do that." She inhaled and nodded. "Nicely browned. Thirty more minutes. No extra coal."

"Thank you." Raimond followed Mrs. Crystal's directions and let her adjust the dials on the brand-new stove. "This is all a surprise for my Emily."

"I knew the original home owner a bit. Do you mind if I take a look at the restoration?"

"Not at all." Raimond swept his hand out to the living room. "If there are any details that are off…"

"It's perfect." She admired the rich floor and stroked the wall's glossy finish. "Better than perfect!"

Raimond checked the food one last time. "What can you tell me about the lady who lived here? Her name wasn't even on the legal documents."

"Her old furniture looks glamorous again. Even the chandelier!" Mrs. Crystal touched a sparkling teardrop. "She was…how shall I say this?"

"Very private?"

"That's a good way to put it. This fireplace just dominates the room."

"I added a personal touch. A marble face imported from France." Raimond knelt down and brushed the hearth. "I saved these old stones. What does this R stand for?"

"I have no idea." Mrs. Crystal sunk into an overstuffed chair. "My neighbor relished being cryptic and mysterious."

"May I offer you a glass of Bordeaux?"

"I couldn't." She watched him uncork and pour a glass. She held out her hand while her eyes wandered the room. "You know, yes I could."

Raimond explained every architectural detail he could remember as she sipped, groaned and took another healthy gulp.

Mrs. Crystal's gaze paused at a bamboo cage hanging from the ceiling. "We've all heard the birds singing for months." She pressed her hand to her chest. "The little darlings, they just glow."

"Also from France." Raimond cleared his throat. "I didn't especially love it there."

"That's hard to believe." Her eyes widened as she took in every detail. "The craftsmen said this was a masterful job, with a keen eye to detail. The home is more beautiful than I remember. Congratulations, Dr. Banitierre."

"*Merci.*"

"Is that?" Mrs. Crystal set her wine glass on the coffee table and flailed at the velvet box on the end table. "That's the ring she wore. I'd recognize it anywhere!"

"The mason found it in the basement when he was repairing the foundation." Raimond handed over the box and watched her hold it up to the firelight. Pulses of force formed an aura around the stone. "Who does it belong to?"

"You, as owner of the estate." She passed it back. "Along with all the power inside."

"Which is what, exactly?" Raimond shrugged at the ring and then at his guest. "Superstition?"

"She never really said. But it always shone, or vibrated, like it is right now." Mrs. Crystal stood. "I appreciate the wine and best of luck with your dinner."

"Thanks to you, I don't need to whisk eggs for an hour and bake a cake." Raimond escorted her to the door. "I'm at work quite a bit, but I'm happy to give tours."

"The ladies may well take you up on the offer." Mrs. Crystal kissed him on both cheeks. "They can be very nosey."

Raimond waited for the door to click shut and slumped against the wall.

At least I've succeeded in fooling all the neighbors with the empty, late night carriages.

He stomped in front of the wall clock with a crooked pendulum and growled. *This antique is an authentic piece of junk.* In a flash he was in the kitchen and back at the dining table. He selected dishes from the corner china cabinet and measured each place setting before adjusting candlesticks and a fresh floral centerpiece.

The knock at the door was faint enough that Raimond thought it was the fireplace logs settling. He continued to rearrange stemware and polish crystal until the knock sounded again.

Who now?

The second he opened the door, the blur of a young woman leapt across the threshold.

"Here I am!" Emily threw her arms around his neck. "Why don't you look happy to see me?"

"I'm ecstatic, Em. I've been waiting all night." Raimond swept her off the floor and kicked the door shut behind him. "Wine, my sweet?"

"Bread, my love?" Emily held up a paper bag. "Fresh from the hospital bakery. I know people."

"I hope you're hungry." Raimond claimed her lips and carried her to the back of the house.

Emily tapped on his shoulders and broke the embrace. "I can't believe this kitchen!" She wiggled until he planted her feet on the shiny floor. "Smells like heaven in here."

"I'm the chef tonight." Raimond plucked the bread from her hand. "Shoo, now."

"Aren't you going to pour me some wine?" She hovered at the edge of the living room until Raimond joined her. "I'm a bit helpless."

"Hardly." Raimond removed the loose cork and poured two glasses with flair. "You're a woman of the world."

Emily raised her glass and clinked it against his. "To us?"

"To our new home and a very special night." Raimond met her crystal goblet and pointed to the table. "Sit."

"Without you?" She settled into the chair.

"Only for a few minutes." Raimond kissed her hair and disappeared into the kitchen. "Dinner is nearly ready."

Emily ran her fingertips over silver scrolls and indigo petals on the china. "May I help?"

"Not necessary. I've got it!"

"Can I look around at least? The work you've done to this place is beautiful."

A frying pan crashed to the ground, taking an avalanche of utensils with it. Raimond bit his lip to keep from swearing. "Go ahead."

Emily slid her chair back and wandered around the perimeter of the room. "Your furniture is immaculate."

"I helped refinish it."

"Fancy rug." She bent down and ran black tassels through her fingers.

"It's a vintage piece—all the way from London."

Emily leaned on a windowsill and inhaled. "Snapdragons and marigolds. Delightful scents of autumn.

"All brand new glass." Raimond bustled out with soup and vegetables. "Come back to the table, so we can eat."

"You never eat." Emily laughed at the towel he waved in her direction. "Moldings look original."

"Re-milled and patched. What do you think of the ceilings?"

"Stamped tin. Charming." She gave a thumbs-up. "Reflects firelight all over the room."

"Can you please sit your perfect bottom on the chair? I've slaved over this meal all night. Look at the time."

"This thing doesn't match the rest of the décor." Emily stuck her tongue out at the old clock. "I've always wanted a big, elegant, grandfather clock."

"Really? You've never mentioned that." Raimond poked his head into the living room and read Emily's smile as a yes. "I've got a clock that will make your jaw drop."

"Is that an extra wine glass?"

"I meant to tell you." Raimond called over his shoulder. "Our neighbor dropped by."

Emily's shoes echoed on the hardwood in the foyer. "May I look upstairs?"

"No." Raimond dropped a lid and zipped around the fireplace. "That's for later, Miss Emily." He jabbed his finger at the dining table and disappeared into the kitchen.

"Oh, my God, yes. Yes, I'll—"

Raimond heard nothing else but silence and Emily's racing heart. "Do you need more wine?"

"Did I ruin the surprise?"

Oh no. He flung the potholders away and staggered through the doorway.

"It was right here, on the mantle." She stood in front of the fireplace, balancing the velvet box in her fingers. "For our special night?"

"Oh, Em." Raimond's legs buckled.

"You don't have to get down on one knee." She handed him the ring and clapped. "Though it's so romantic."

Raimond felt the floor against his shin. *How the hell did this happen?*

"Yes—I mean." Emily made a zipping motion across her lips. "I'll wait 'til you ask."

He searched his mind for the right words. *Any words.*

"Take your time." She fidgeted with her dress.

"Miss Emily Gastrell." Raimond cleared his throat. "Do you have any plans for the next…seventy years?"

"I do not." She bounced on her toes. "Not yet, anyway."

"Then, will you do me the honor—" Raimond took her hands, kissed both her knuckles and looked straight up into her eyes, "—of becoming my wife?"

"Yes, yes!" Emily hauled him to his feet and wiggled the fingers of her left hand. "I want to wear it!"

Raimond fumbled with the ring and dropped the box. Her tiny hand stopped trembling as the ring slid over porcelain skin as if drawn in by her heart. The emerald's sparkle was only outshone by her jubilant smile.

This time, Raimond was ready for Emily's jump into his arms.

"I love you. I love you." Emily buried her face in his neck. "I love you Raimond Banitierre. For the rest of my life."

With the candles burning and all the other lights in the dining area dimmed, Raimond finally served the meal.

"Who taught you how to set such a gorgeous table?" Emily shook her head slowly. "This is more silverware than I've ever seen. What do I do with all the glasses?"

"My mother loved to entertain on the holidays." Raimond adjusted the steaming plates in perfect symmetry and pointed to each piece of crystal. "Red wine, white wine or champagne, and water. For the silverware, work from the outside to the inside."

"Salad?" Emily picked up a fork and flipped it over.

"In France the tines face down. Yes, that's for salad and the next one—"

Emily seized the bigger fork, stabbed it into a carrot and popped it in her mouth. "Oh, that's delicious!"

Raimond touched the back of his hand to his cheek and whisked away droplets of pink.

"Oh no! I've never seen you—" Emily grabbed his hand. "Did I use the wrong fork?"

"You're just so lovely." Raimond leaned forward and showered her hand with kisses. "I don't care what fork you use or if you eat with your fingers. You've made me the happiest man in the world."

Emily dug into the meal as if she hadn't eaten in a week.

I could have planned a better proposal than that. All the excuses Raimond had prepared about not actually sharing the food went unused. *At least she said yes, but that ring. I know nothing about it except legally...Emily already owned it.*

"Scrumptious." She motioned to the turkey. "You'll have to teach me how to use the new oven."

"I did have a bit of help." Raimond sipped wine. "Full disclosure, the extra glass you saw belonged to the neighbor."

"Oh yes, I forgot." Emily nodded to the coffee table. "Was she nice? Was she pretty?"

"Very pleasant, and quite a bit older than me." Raimond hid his smirk with a linen napkin. "She stopped by and I let her assist me with that behemoth in the kitchen."

"Well, that was very sweet."

"She also brought your favorite pie."

"Pecan? Now, I know I'll like her." Emily stood to clear the table and clucked as he caught her wrist. "You can't stop me, fiancé. But you may help."

Raimond scooped up a few plates and followed her into the kitchen. "Em, wait." He tugged on her sleeve until she placed the china in the sink. "I just wanted to tell you..."

"Tell me anything." Emily wrapped her arms around his back and pressed her chest against his. "Tell me everything."

He kissed her lips. "I can't wait to be your husband."

"When was the last time we danced?" Emily spun in his arms, placed her hand on his shoulder and straightened her back. "We may need to practice before our wedding."

"What will it be, fiancée?" Raimond held out his palm.

Emily walked her delicate fingers down his outstretched arm. "A waltz?"

He slid his hand around her waist. "The waltz it is."

"Right here in the kitchen?" She glided back and to the side. "With no music?"

Raimond leaned in and began to hum, drawing Emily across the floor with elegant movements. Her voice joined his and they floated to the melody.

This engagement was a surprise. He stood back and twirled her twice before stepping close again. *But it's perfect. She's perfect.* A faint noise in the garden forced his attention over her shoulder and through the window without breaking step. *Almost feels like eyes on me.*

"May we have pie now?"

"Certainly." Raimond stopped in the middle of the floor with a flourish.

"I'll cut two slices."

If those nosey ladies are watching us dance... Raimond rummaged in the silverware drawer and searched the darkness. *We put on quite a show.*

"Do you have more forks?" Emily swished to the dining room.

"Only one." He yanked heavy drapes across the window. "May I feed you pecans?"

"Of course, my love."

"I still need to explain things." Raimond took three giant steps and pulled her back into his chest. "I've been promising you forever."

"Love tonight. Explain tomorrow. And I want to hear all about that mystery clock." Emily kissed his lips. "Praise the angels!"

Chapter 19

UNHOLY MISCALCULATION

RAIMOND LET ONE eye drift open to watch Emily fuss with pots of lipstick on her antique dressing table and brush pearl powder on her cheeks. The strap of her nightgown slipped off her shoulder, exposing glowing skin and the gentle curve of her breast.

"I know you're watching."

"You know no such thing." He rolled onto his side. "Tell me again why you're going to work on your day off. At dinnertime?"

"Hopefully it's only for a few hours." She reread a handwritten note delivered by the courier and tossed it to him. "Some sort of emergency meeting. Not sure why you didn't receive the same message."

"I'm just the new fellow." Raimond shrugged and crumpled the paper into a ball. "I'll send my carriage and if you aren't home by eight, I'll come looking. I know the neighborhood has grown and the new sidewalks nearly reach our cottage but darkness falls early at this time of year. Please don't wander about alone."

"You worry too much." Emily sighed as she twisted the green sparkle off her finger. "You need to hold onto this for now. I can't be seen wearing it. Not yet."

"It will be in the velvet box on the mantle, where you first found it." He reluctantly took the ring. "Unless you've changed your mind?"

Emily finished dressing, bathed in sunset's leftover glow as it streamed through the stained glass. She checked her reflection in the mirror and leaned across the bed to kiss Raimond good-bye. "My answer remains a resounding yes." She pressed her lips to his cheek. "Yes, yes, yes."

"That's all I get? A peck on the cheek?"

She tugged on the tall collar of her nursing uniform. "Feeling a bit frumpy."

"You're a vision." Raimond sat up and gathered her into his arms. "Wish I could walk you to the hospital."

"You're not going out in public like this." The back of her hand trailed down his bare chest. "I'd have to beat the ladies off with a stick."

"We need to finish the conversation we started last night, and the three nights before that." Raimond pressed his lips to her knuckles. "You need to know—"

"What I'm getting into? I know you used to be a soldier in France. And something bad happened."

"It's a complicated story that must be told all at once." He flopped back on the bed.

Emily curled into his arms and nibbled his earlobe. "But we keep getting distracted."

Raimond tried not to laugh. "All your fault, *mademoiselle*."

Emily giggled and kissed his lips. "I didn't realize there was still fighting in France."

"There hasn't been for many years." His face went blank. "Please, skip this absurd meeting. Stay here with me so I can explain everything."

"I'll make it quick." She jumped up and straightened her skirt. "Promise."

"Take your shawl." Raimond reached for purple fabric woven with glimmer. He clutched her fingers when he handed it over. "I love you."

"Your kooky birds are chirping like crazy."

"I don't know what's gotten into them recently. Maybe they're tired of Augusta. I'll have them figured out and fluttering all over the house when you get home."

"Beating my head with their wings." Emily blew him a kiss and hurried into the fading dusk. "Love you, always."

"Always."

At eight o'clock sharp, Raimond stopped in the street and focused on the dark windows of Emily's rooming house. She wasn't there and only a skeleton staff was at the hospital when he checked in. If there had been an emergency meeting, it was long over and no one was talking about it. The silence of the nighttime corridors had an odd vibe, as if the quiet was the peace before a spider's nest of eggs exploded. The carriage he sent sat, unused, on the corner.

I'll bet she went for an evening stroll. He set out for the cottage on foot. *The lady has a mind of her own, but Augusta isn't what it used to be.*

Several times over the past weeks, Raimond sensed the time to leave had arrived. They had pushed their secret long enough. If Emily wound up humiliated by judgmental church folk, they would have stayed one night too long. She didn't deserve such treatment. Though his marriage proposal was unexpected, it was complete with wine, flowers, a vintage emerald ring and his genuine love. Even her wedding present, the clock Aveline had rescued from the basement of Chambord, was repaired and hidden in the garden shed.

Maybe a Lord exists for every being, human or monster. My parents, may they rest in peace, would have believed it. In the eyes of that supreme power, they were already blessed and it was no accident that she was his fiancée.

Legal obstacles over the Savannah home Raimond inherited had finally been settled. The deceased owner's name, the identity of his first real patient, would remain on the property documents until he married Emily. Then it would all belong to her. The old estate was in poor repair, but workers had already begun cutting back the overgrown grounds. With a woman's touch, the plantation's southern glory would shine through like the day it was built. He kicked weedy dandelions in the sidewalk cracks and stroked pure tropical specimens overhanging formal gardens.

The marvelous dichotomy of life.

Both thrived within inches of each other. He dismissed the first lifeless bird he encountered as the normal cycle of nature. A growing trail of ruined feathers made him freeze in his tracks. A peculiar fog swirled around his feet. Beside his boot, he recognized the jeweled and metallic threads of a discarded shawl. *When did she drop this?* Raimond's gaze was dragged up and drawn to an eerie glow. The acrid stench of smoke slammed into him like a cannonball.

Behind a wall of trees that swayed and flailed like wounded victims begging for help, his cottage was engulfed in fire.

"No, no, no!" Raimond shot toward the inferno. White flames danced with abandon amidst heavy black air. "Emily!"

The front door was completely consumed, as if the blaze had originated there. Sparks zipped up the flowering vines like fuses, on a mission to ignite the roof. He raced around the back, ignoring ragged glass that exploded from every window like a hail of bullets. The kitchen door stood ajar, Emily's beaded purse lay open on the threshold. The chain was twisted, fragmented and stained with blood. Raimond flashed past the hulking cobalt oven toward the dining room door. "Emily!"

Standing on the hearth, oblivious to the flames, a translucent shape fumbled with a box on the mantle. Emerald rays illuminated a familiar profile that rippled like liquid velvet, but when the thing turned to him, a face with no features.

"I'm here, I'm coming!" Raimond braced himself for searing pain as he dove into the blaze but was repelled by an impenetrable barrier that roiled like molten steel. "Em, run to me! I'll heal you!" The figure tipped its head and then gazed up, as if a stronger voice beckoned from the sky. Without acknowledging Raimond's cries again, the phantom climbed the river rock of the fireplace like a ladder, vanishing into the hell above. "Emily!" Every attempt he made to breach the inferno, hurtled him farther away, until he fell, unconscious in the neighboring corn field.

When he woke the flames had died and the smoke was replaced by a foul vulgar haze. Raimond forced himself to stay hidden while a stranger held his hand over the pile of rubble and ash that used to be his home. A holy man made the sign of the cross in the air. The moment the priest cleared the space, Raimond dashed into what remained of his parlor, combing the debris for signs of life. He found nothing but the well-hidden entrance to a basement that didn't exist on any house plans. The surface was scorched, but with only minutes before sunrise he scrambled into the blackness. A heavy door slammed shut, showering his face with ashes, wreckage and a solid object that hit him as if thrown by a furious hand.

The diary. How in the world did this survive? Raimond brushed off soot to reveal red leather and silver trim. He pressed the book to his lips and let dry sobs wrack his body. *Aveline, I miss you terribly. Now, I fear I've lost my beloved Emily too.*

Chapter 20

HAUNTED

NIGHT AFTER NIGHT, Raimond didn't move a muscle while Emily's scent overpowered him in the steady rain.

What if that phantom I saw wasn't her?

Sickly sweet needles of terror and agony made the truth harsh and clear.

My beautiful girl burned to death in this damn house.

With only his experimental bourbon vials and his diary for company, each day Raimond allowed himself to remain paralyzed and trapped in the secret compartment, he flirted with being discovered. He didn't recognize the voice of the priest who appeared every evening to chant peculiar prayers over the wrecked cottage.

All I've done has been for nothing. What's the point of existing anymore?

Even when Raimond lay silent through countless sunrises and sunsets, his mind never stopped spinning, revisiting careless miscalculations and fatal mistakes. The only movement in the subterranean chamber was an unconscious flex of the vampire's right arm, directing spelled wine to his lips.

The birds. How did I miss the birds' warning?

He didn't realize the priest's nightly visits and unintelligible Latin mumblings had dwindled until his grasp found nothing but broken bottles and a stockpile of blood-wine run dry. Raimond's eyes finally snapped open and demented truth drowned his mind.

Now it all makes revolting sense.

He bolted straight up, choking on his own tongue.

That fire was intentional and never about the church or improper sexual relations outside of marriage.

Someone stumbled upon a secret much more damaging than tarnished virtue.

Demons. But they blamed Emily and not me.

Thinking back on the men who accompanied the priest during his early visits, Raimond's soul shrieked and trembled.

That priest.

Emily had been lured to the emergency hospital meeting like prey. When she ran, they chased her and caught her in his house.

Where is that unholy bastard?

Raimond shoved the compartment door up and it hardly budged. It took all his strength to dislodge the hatch. He slithered out, one limb at a time, to find inches of moss and debris weighing it down.

When did all this pile up?

The air was stagnant and devoid of life. Not one footprint marred the slick muck surrounding the cottage's crumbling foundation. The scarcely lingering scent of human blood turned Raimond's head north, toward the wilderness lakes. He stumbled and caught himself on the rusted hulk that had once been Emily's new oven. Staggering through the garden, he stopped to peek through peeling shed doors still secured by the original padlock. In the middle of oddly clean darkness, a hulking object sat draped in a perfectly pressed sheet.

First thing tomorrow, I'm shipping that damn clock back to Scotland.

With the night stretching out before him and a nagging ache in his gut, he half walked and half ran toward the encampments along the Savannah River. It took hours and more than a few breaks to gather his strength until he found the first outpost. Before ducking through the rustic tavern's front door, he dipped a rag into a watering trough and scoured grime from his face. He wrung it out and scrubbed his loose skin three more times before the cloth came away clean.

Feed first. Ask questions later.

Raimond drove his hand up through soil so dense that it collapsed back in on itself faster than he could dig his way out.

How did I sink so deep?

His thrashing arms finally broke through to the surface and he spit out mud mixed with rotted bark as he climbed onto the forest floor.

Last thing I remember, I was hiding in a hollowed out fallen tree in sweltering heat.

Frost crackled under his feet and he looked through leafless trees to a crisp, winter moon.

The weather in Georgia has gone crazy. But now I have no doubt that the priest who chanted over my cottage was a wicked freak with no rightful claim to the cloth. The murderer will pay, as will the charlatans in his camp.

Raimond focused his vengeful gaze on the smoking chimneys and towering steeple of a settlement on the peninsula.

They've been conspiring with the criminal all along, and by the looks of that fancy chapel, prospering.

He leaned against a tree and fought to control spasming in his chest. A thick crimson haze clouded his vision while white-hot air forced its way into his lungs. His mind replayed Emily's last kiss over and over, until he charged down the hill and leapt over the encampment wall.

By the time Raimond staggered back to the icy grove, he was drenched in blood. No chimneys smoked in the village below and the church was missing a chunk of its steeple.

Not since the darkest days in Paris…

He dropped to his knees and let out a guttural roar.

Arrogant imbeciles. But they gave the truth up in the end.

Tonight, the fake priest would make his yearly visit.

Raimond took a last look at the silent village.

I left no witnesses.

He swallowed back acid and bile, banishing the gory scene to the deepest recesses of his mind and made a final trek back to Augusta. He swept through the ruined cottage, found his diary and tucked it into a secret pocket.

It's like nobody ever lived here.

He still cursed the fact that none of his textbooks were salvageable, not even his medical school diploma. Worst of all, he didn't have enough of Emily's remains to grant her a proper burial.

One decisive task remains. Then I'll greet the sunrise and let my story end.

As midnight fell on the anniversary of Emily's death, a priest arrived to chant his phony blessing, alone and unguarded. Raimond didn't even attempt to hide.

"Father." Raimond blasted out from the double chimney's moonlit shadow. "Looking for someone?"

The man took a step back and smoothed the scarlet vestment around his neck. He squinted at Raimond's silhouette and the empty space behind him. "Your name, sir?"

"Dr. Raimond—"

"Banitierre? I see you've been ill." The priest exhaled and let his shoulders drop. "But the hospital will be so relieved to hear you've survived…this."

"They think I've died?" Raimond arched one eyebrow.

"Yes, Doctor," the priest whispered. "All those years ago, in the hell fire."

How damn long has it been? Raimond battled back anguish as fresh and devastating as the night of the tragedy. "The seminary taught you to burn innocents? Oh, wait." He flashed in front of the priest. "You didn't graduate from any holy institution, did you?"

"Merciful Lord." The priest fumbled with the pocket of his robe and scrambled away from Raimond's hollow, searing red eyes. "Deliver me from—"

"Don't bother begging a Lord you don't serve." Raimond grasped the man's throat and lifted him up by his throat. "What's in your pocket? Show me!"

The man's shaky hand produced a pistol. "I was almost a priest, once."

"But you chose devilry over the cloth."

"I was found unfit…by idiots." He fumbled with the trigger. "They gave me no choice."

"Drop it." Raimond shook him like a rag doll and the gun skittered across the stone floor. "Now, tell me what happened to my Emily."

"They suspected she was—" He covered his face. "A witch."

Raimond squeezed his neck tighter. "Why?"

The man kicked as he dug his nails into Raimond's wrist. "There was a little boy." He gasped for breath. "She cursed him."

"You mean Freddie? He lived."

"Should have died, they said. The witch defied the Lord."

"I healed that child. Me!" Raimond hissed. "Who suspected her?"

"Church—hospital—hired me to exorcise a demon."

"They trusted an incompetent." Raimond dropped him in a heap.

"The scent of magic was all over her. Your scent." The man slid back rubbing his throat. "You're presumed dead. I'll keep that secret, I'll even give you blood."

"Filthy killer." Raimond ripped the white tab out of the fake priest's collar. "I wouldn't drink from you if you were the last human on earth."

"Then what do you want?" He didn't wait for an answer but bolted for the street.

"Revenge." Raimond caught him by the scarlet cloth around his neck. He twisted it and yanked him back. "And the ring you stole."

"I stole nothing." The man's eyes bulged as his face swelled. "I swear it!"

"Liar." Raimond wrenched him around and twisted the scarf tighter. "Repent, and I'll make this quick."

"I might be a fallen priest, but I'll never bend my knee to a son of Satan."

"That's who you think I am? So be it." Raimond plunged his hand into the man's chest and sluggishly removed his heart. Though his eyes fluttered with the agony, he didn't lose consciousness until the last vessel was torn free. *No witnesses.* Raimond tossed the bloody mess into the old fireplace, lit a match and watched it burn. *No evidence.*

For an hour after the flames went out, Raimond stood motionless in the gloom, waiting for a flood of relief. He finally moved and destroyed what was left of the chimneys, smashing his fists into brittle brick and mortar. He still didn't feel any closure or peace, only the crushing shame of taking another life.

Shaky prayer broke the silence. "Hail Mary, full of grace."

Raimond spun and searched the darkness until a woman stepped across the tangle of weeds that used to be Emily's prized flower bed. He ducked and crawled behind a pile of stones with no safe path to his hidden door. *How long has she been standing there?*

The woman coughed and gagged as a rogue gust delivered the stench of freshly burned flesh. "Hail Holy Queen, Mother of Mercy."

Mother Superior? This was all her fault. Raimond peeked around at the hunched kneeling nun. He felt his skin sizzle while fangs throbbed in his gums. *She's much more frail than I remember.*

"I bless the memory of a beautiful girl I failed to save, and a gifted doctor we lost far too young." Mother Superior laid two bouquets of flowers in the ashes. She precisely dropped a card in the rubble before yanking the veil from her head. Thin grey hair drooped over her sunken, tear-stained cheeks. She crossed her heart with a bony hand and limped down the pitch-black road.

How many damn years has it been? Raimond half flashed and half crawled to the bouquets and unearthed the worn metal lid of a buried box. He pulled out a pile of handwritten notes signed by Mother Superior and rifled through the jumble until he found the most current date. *October twenty-ninth, 1899.*

Raimond's hand fell limp and the paper fluttered in the breeze. All the grief and anger he'd felt the second before drained away. *No one else dies tonight. Not even me.* He slumped onto the dirty stones and lay back in the ashes to stare at the night sky. *It's my duty to assure this never happens again.* His right hand brushed against something smooth and familiar under the shattered bricks. He rolled over to find the faceted bottle of blood bourbon.

Must be magic in this elixir after all. Raimond held it up to the fleeting moonlight and groaned. *Though I don't recall drinking so much of it.*

Clouds eclipsed the moon and crumbling bricks shifted to erase the bottle's void.

"Dearest Emily, you'll never be forgotten." He sipped and crossed his heart. "I will forever bear the guilt of this tragedy."

PART III
NEW ORLEANS

Chapter 21

THE ACCUSATION

RAIMOND LAY ON his back in a polished crate borrowed from a furniture warehouse. Instead of a grand piano, tonight a vampire was riding in cushioned luxury. When the rails beneath him turned from smooth, new steel of post-war reconstruction to the familiar rickety joints, Raimond nudged the lid open. He crawled out in time to see the scenery change from coastal plain to boggy swamp. This boxcar on the midnight train from Augusta would carry him close enough to reach his Savannah hospital, the last place he remembered feeling safe and happy, but he would have to hurry to outrun the dawn.

I've been gone from that city and my friends for far too long.

A carved totem pole marked the corner of an abandoned rice plantation and his signal to exit. He jumped from the rolling train and flashed for the safety of the stately columned mansion that would have been Emily's home. Under the slate of the old fireplace, Raimond found two stashed wine bottles. He tucked one under his arm, tore the cork out of the other with his fangs and poured the blood cocktail down his throat. He stiffened at whispers in his ears and a faint pulse of power, but they vanished in a second.

Like the cobwebs of that damn Chambord. After tucking his ancient bourbon under the hearth, he strode across the old parlor. *At least they didn't deliver that depressing clock here. Must be at the Port of Savannah. Good riddance.* He peeked through broken shutters at a brightening sky and headed for the front door.

Both bottles skittered across the wooden porch as Raimond was slammed down. He fought off two cloaked attackers until he was standing again. Three more strangers wrestled him into submission. Even with one assailant's heel crushing his face into the rotting deck, he managed to reach for the wine. The tips of his fingers sent the bottle rolling until a gleaming boot stopped it on the edge of the steps. Raimond's eyes followed spotless trouser pants up to the braided detail of a scarlet jacket. The distant pulse exploded into the drone of ten million bees.

"Commander Raimond Banitierre." A blond vampire crossed his arms with precision and flaunted a crisp smirk. "You, sir, are under arrest for treason."

Time varied between speeding and crawling as Raimond drifted in and out of consciousness. When he slept, he dreamt of glowing birds that pecked at his eyes until he went blind. During his waking hours, he fought the agony of burning gold chains by focusing on figures and scenes painted on the crumbling ceiling tiles of his unconventional prison. *Should have let them kill me.* A commotion in the darkness beyond dragged him back to reality.

"Wake up, prisoner." A soldier slid a canteen across the worn floorboards. "Your daily allotment."

"Daily?" Raimond fought his mind's flashback of a Paris prison and Faison's henchmen doling out miniscule rations. He drank the contents of the container in one gulp. "Tasty. Wild boar?"

"You don't even deserve that, criminal." A guard with decorated uniform sleeves and a chest full of medals lunged at him. "I should—"

"Halt!"

The temperature in the old building plummeted. Outside, even the crickets' song was cut off as if they all choked at once.

Both soldiers dropped back and mumbled. "Yes, Your Highness."

"You may stand down." The blond man with the gleaming boots strode past worn velvet chairs and stomped onto the raised stage. "I'll take it from here."

"Who are you?" Raimond tossed the flask aside. "You have no right to hold me here."

The decorated soldier flashed forward. "Do you live under a rock? He's the son of King—"

"Commander Banitierre, meet Captain Karl." The blond shoved the guard away. "Kindly allow me to handle this."

The captain cursed under his breath.

"Ignore him." The stranger smoothed invisible wrinkles out of his coat. "He's my father's man."

Raimond leapt against his restraints. "Who the hell are you?"

"*The* Crown Prince of North America, Draven Norman." The prince stood his ground as Raimond's shackles yanked him to a stop inches in front of his face. "Charmed to make your acquaintance."

A masked wave of force shot from Draven's palm, drove Raimond back as far as the chains allowed and slammed him into the floor hard enough to splinter the old planks.

Raimond dabbed black blood from his nose and tried to stand.

"You'd be wise to stay put." Draven's voice dripped ice. "Likely a few shattered bones."

"I demand to hear the charges against me."

"Again?"

Raimond snarled, "If you've nothing else more pressing."

"We've received corroborated testimony that you murdered the miserable Faison of Paris."

"Over thirty years ago." Raimond let his body sag to the floor. "*Je suis coupable.*"

"Guilt or innocence will be judged by me." Draven strode across the stage. "I am intrigued, however, to learn *why* you did it."

Raimond spent the next few hours explaining how he had died and woken up an enslaved demon at the hands of Faison.

"Chambord?" Draven leaned forward and hung on every detail of the battle at the castle. "Wait, your Aveline found what?"

"An old clock...magnificently preserved, but heavy as a—"

"*The* clock?" Draven's grey eyes sparkled. "We'll talk more about that later. Do continue."

Raimond launched into the saga of his medical training but faltered and struggled for the words to explain Emily's death.

"My condolences on the loss of your fiancée."

"I hold myself completely responsible for that catastrophe. I still feel like walking into the sun."

"I know we've been acquainted for mere hours, but you strike me as a man who might find a better way to honor his fallen love."

"*Oui.*" Raimond's head fell into his hands. "My death would make her furious."

"So, simply don't do it. Tell me more of Faison. You say he had tattoos?"

"All over his arms and chest." Raimond cringed. "And they moved under his skin as if they were alive."

"I have to ask you to keep that a secret from the others." Draven clenched and unclenched his fists. "I've only heard of the living ink in clandestine legend. My instinct is hinting that it should stay there."

"I haven't told anyone this story since..." Raimond raked his hands through his long hair. "Ever."

"Of this entire sordid tale," Draven tapped his cheek, "so far, I'm most disturbed by the involvement of German witches in your assassination."

"Honestly, I find Faison's cruelty to children much worse." Raimond fought a wave of queasiness. "Barbaric behavior."

"Unthinkable." Draven snapped his fingers. An impeccably dressed butler appeared with two silver chalices of blood. "You need to drink. No wildlife this time."

"I have a policy against—" The scent was overpowering. Raimond seized the cup with both his chained hands and drained it dry.

Draven raised an eyebrow and sipped his own drink. "Finish that statement."

"I don't kill, just to feed. It's unnecessary, plus I took an oath to preserve human life."

"Noble." Draven shrugged one shoulder and raised a palm to the ceiling. "Somewhat foolish."

"How did you find me after all this time? Was it my visits to the river encampments?"

"Besides the fact you didn't bother to change your name?" Draven chuckled. "No, you disguised those attacks quite convincingly. It was mostly the last village, where you ripped off heads."

Raimond rattled the gold cuff clamped to his wrist. "But I put them back—"

"On the wrong people."

"*Je suis fini.*" Raimond's eyes rolled back and his body wilted, shuddering from the inside out.

"Oh stop, you aren't ruined." Draven fiddled with his cufflinks. "It happens."

"You may think I'm a hypocrite, but those villagers were concealing the false, murdering priest."

"Hunger you may be able to control, but anger is a brutal beast. Honestly, I'm relieved you aren't perfect." Draven finished his drink and let the chalice drop. "That would make me look unscrupulous."

"I assume I'll have to stand trial."

"Much as you've swayed me with your account, it is vampire law. My father sent me here to preside. I believe it's his version of a royal test, so I can't go home without a proper verdict."

"Is there iron-clad proof?"

"Faison's henchmen, your accusers, provided sworn statements in blood." Draven motioned to the captain, standing at the edge of darkness. "Unlock his cuffs."

"Your Highness?" Karl hesitated.

"He's not running away." Draven fused his eyes with Raimond's. "Are you?"

"I promise, I will not. Since you have signed documents, I assume we'll start immediately?"

"Never mind that he's been running for decades." Karl sneered. "We'll trust him at his word."

Draven ignored Karl's outburst. "Are there any vampires of your bloodline that would testify in your defense?"

"I don't..." Raimond shrugged. "Like who?"

"Vampires you've turned or those with sworn loyalty to your blood."

"There are none. I never...I'm completely alone."

"That is bewildering, and dreadfully inaccurate. The paperwork is in order now, but so help me..." The prince massaged his temples. "Several living witnesses have come forward and requested the proceedings be delayed until tomorrow night."

Raimond rubbed his burned wrists and shook his head. "Why?"

"At great risk of stating the obvious," Draven pointed to a hole in the grand roof before stalking away, "you will be tried for treason by the light of a full, bloody moon."

Chapter 22
COURT OF OPPOSITES

RAIMOND PACED HIS prison of worn floorboards all day, finding shredded curtains and rusted pulleys in the wings. He paused on each faded chalk line, wondering what inspired roles the actors had been playing when they stood on those marks. Broken gas lamps formed a jagged railing at the edge facing the vacant hall. He slumped into a chair and looked straight up at a noose of frayed rope drifting in the musty breeze.

What a perfect place for a trial. The haunted stage in a theater of the macabre.

As dusk melted through the Savannah swamp, commotion bubbled up from the vaults and burst into the gallery. Vampire soldiers filed in, carrying furniture and the trappings of a courtroom. Human footmen followed with jugs of water, piles of fresh linen and a garment rack.

Raimond's blank stare landed on a perfect line of men, just below the border of the stage. "Is this parade part of the legal proceedings?"

Draven swept down the aisle. "Local residents I've convinced to assist. The grander, the better. Make yourself presentable." He pointed to the clothing. "Find something in that collection that fits."

Raimond scanned the hangers. "So my choices are dull black or dismal grey? Am I a condemned man already?"

"You're the defendant." Draven dismissed him to focus on workers fabricating a royal court in a decrepit venue. "And cheer up, every piece is either Italian silk or cashmere. The latter, I stole from under the nose of a psychotic Himalayan king."

Within an hour, Raimond emerged in an onyx suit and matching shirt pinstriped with smoke. In the light of blazing torches, his hair reflected the shades of black and hung long enough to brush his shoulders.

"Nice to see you shaved." Draven shifted on his carved wooden throne, tapping one foot and sipping whisky from crystal. "Any more complaints?"

"That I'm fighting for my cursed life instead of saving those of the innocent."

"Exceptionally dramatic. Shall we begin?" Draven held out his right palm. When none of his company moved, he repeated the motion with emphasis. "My gavel!" With the implement in his hand, he searched for somewhere to use it. He finally rapped it on the arm of his seat. "Just…carry on."

"Commander Raimond Banitierre is officially charged with the murder of Faison of Paris, France," Captain Karl declared. "High treason against the Norman empire."

"I prefer Doctor," Raimond said.

"As if anyone cares." The captain unrolled parchments and read each document out loud, along with the signatures of the accusers. "I recommend we declare him guilty and proceed to the execution immediately."

Raimond's chest seized and blood roared in his ears.

"Don't play stupid, soldier." The captain adjusted his coat to show Raimond a gold dagger hanging from his belt. "You know the penalty for treason."

"The most important document of all is this book." Draven held Faison's ledger open. "The name, Raimond Banitierre, is in sacred ink as legitimate offspring."

"Damning proof of patricide, at least." The captain laughed in Raimond's face. "Off with his miserable head."

"This will be a proper trial." The prince wielded his gavel with enough force to splinter the chair's arm. "Karl, must I, yet again, remind you of your station?"

"Your Highness, I was assigned this task by your father."

"My father," Draven echoed.

"Yes, and in light of the family's current issues—"

"You must be referring to my scandalously incompetent brother whom you served, or mis-served, for years." Draven slid forward. "I've been appointed as heir to the throne."

"And the sooner this is finished, the sooner we can return home."

"My home, Karl," Draven hissed. "I'd like nothing more than to leave you here, in this foul swamp."

"Your father's blood would boil."

"His blood is my blood." Draven leapt from his makeshift throne. "Not yours!"

"I—" Karl tipped his chin up and pounded his chest, "—am a Norman too."

"From some wretched, watered down, minor lineage. We don't create offspring to staff the common military." Draven flung his gavel at Karl.

The captain ducked in plenty of time, but the wooden hammer struck a young valet in the forehead, sending him sailing backward. A loud crack rang through the theater as his face struck the metal frame of a seat.

"My son!" A human in a servant's livery raced to the boy's side. Blood gushed from the boy's nose as his eyes rolled back. "You promised you wouldn't harm us."

"Gentlemen, enough!" Raimond flashed from the stage, wrestling his way past vampires clamoring toward the boy. "This child requires medical attention. I'll need someone to fetch my medical bag."

Draven strode to the front of the mob and grabbed Karl by his decorated collar. "You heard the good doctor. Retrieve his bag."

"And where would that bag be located?" Karl growled.

"In the farmhouse where you attacked me."

"You expect me to slog through the countryside?" Karl ripped Draven's hands off his shirt. "It's a mile away, at least."

"The bag is on the shelf above the mantle." Raimond held towels to the boy's wound. "I don't care who goes."

Draven tipped his chin and raised his hand. Hidden power sent Karl hurtling across the theater into the balcony's façade. The ever-present scent of mold grew stronger.

The captain crawled from splinters of rotted seats and re-adjusted his uniform. "You've certainly inherited the fabled Norman temper."

"Fetch the damn bag, Karl!" Draven turned back to Raimond, pushing salivating monsters away from the bloody scene. "What can I do to help?"

"Hand me some more clean linen." Raimond dabbed at the boy's wound. "Luckily, this won't need sutures."

Draven jammed another towel in Raimond's outstretched hand, flicked the bloody one away with his boot and covered his mouth. "How do you tolerate the smell?"

"Concentrate on the patient, in this case, an innocent child." Raimond caught the medical bag hurled at him from a disgruntled Karl. "That was quick, thank you, sir."

Karl kicked red mud off his boots and grunted.

"Will my son recover?" A frail man knelt next to Raimond. "He's all the family I've got left."

"A scary injury to be sure, but not fatal. He may have black eyes from the broken nose and quite a headache, but at his age, he'll be up and asking for dinner in no time." Raimond finished cleaning blood from the boy's face and began applying gauze and a wrap to hold it in place. "The Prince regrets his actions."

Karl's jaw dropped.

The muscles in Draven's neck twitched. "Do I?"

"Are you a savage?" Raimond stared at him and time stood still. "Your Highness?"

Draven shrugged a shoulder and met the father's eyes. "I sincerely—"

"I'm hungry." The boy reached for his face.

"You see?" Raimond guided his hands away.

"Thank you, kind sir." The boy's father gathered his son in a hug and gently rocked back and forth. "Thank you."

Karl snorted into the collar of his coat. "Pitiful."

"What's your favorite food, lad?" Raimond asked.

"May I have bread?"

"Find bread," Draven barked at his guards. "Now!"

In minutes they returned, empty handed. "No bread in the building, Your Highness."

"Captain Karl, don't you keep a few chocolates in your pocket?" Draven tipped his head.

"They're from Vienna." Karl reluctantly produced a muslin pouch of individually wrapped candies. "Fine, take them."

"Then chocolate it is." Raimond took a piece and handed it to the boy. *"Merci beaucoup, Karl."*

Draven smirked. "Don't be rude, Captain."

"You're welcome." Karl rolled his eyes and bowed. "Dr. Banitierre."

Draven turned away and walked to the base of the stage while the theater was cleared of all but the essential participants. Before he climbed the battered steps and re-took the wooden throne, he hissed in Raimond's ear, "To any of the mundane creatures in attendance, this is a conventional court at an unconventional hour."

Raimond nodded.

"Can we please continue this charade?" Karl rested his hands on his knees. "So, it may be finished."

"As soon as you light the official flame." Draven pointed to a crooked cauldron at centerstage. "Try not to burn the building down."

"It's a dump." Karl tossed a match into the iron vessel.

"Take your places everyone." Draven sat back and surveyed the audience. "Raimond, you've heard the charges."

"I plead—"

"Silence." Draven banged his gavel. "You'll do no such thing without proper counsel."

"I never considered…" Raimond held his palms out. "Where would I find—"

"Right here." The tap of a cane preceded the entrance of a well-dressed gentleman.

"Benjamin? You're a long way from Savannah." Raimond rushed to help the elderly man down the aisle. "Surely you don't realize what you've volunteered for or how different I am from you."

"I was your patient for years. Without you, I'd be crippled or dead." Benjamin beckoned a young soldier to bring a chair. "And I'm aware of what you are."

Raimond raised his brow. "I very much hope not."

Benjamin leaned closer and whispered. "The rest just worship the ground you walk on."

"I knew of your military service and that you were wounded in combat." Raimond straightened the ribbons on Benjamin's chest. "The War of 1812?"

"Not just any combat, The Battle of New Orleans. Afterward, I followed in my father's footsteps and went to law school." Benjamin unbuttoned his azure uniform coat and lowered himself into the formal seat. "I spent years in the office of the Judge Advocate General. This proceeding has court-martial written all over it."

"Who authorized a—this person—to participate in Norman business?" Karl stomped across the stage until he stood in front of Raimond and his lawyer. "Stop whispering and conspiring. This outsider needs to leave immediately!"

"Karl," Draven said. "Either shut your mouth, or *you* will become the eternal outsider."

Benjamin leaned on his cane and stood to his full height. "Dr. Banitierre pleads not guilty by reason of self-defense and the defense of others in imminent danger."

"So, he admits it!" Karl spun around and forced his body to freeze. "I apologize, Your Highness."

"We're well aware that Faison was a treacherous outlaw." Draven's glare shot from Karl to Raimond. "How many others did said outlaw murder?"

"Hundreds," Raimond answered. "Not only my soldiers, but women, toddlers, infants…the ones he didn't kill, he tortured so heinously that death would have been a blessing."

"Can you prove that?" Draven asked.

Raimond focused on Benjamin and shook his head.

"And the night of this crime? The incident I'm to pass judgement on?" Draven leaned forward. "Was Faison a direct threat to you?"

"After you chased him and ambushed him in an abandoned castle, he means?" Karl pretended to examine his sword.

"We fought to the death. I had absolutely no choice. His guards killed one of my sisters—the nurse Aveline."

"Any witnesses?"

"Unfortunately, I sailed to America alone."

Draven gave an impatient wave and a door in the back of the theater squeaked on its hinges. "Not entirely."

Raimond peered up the aisle and his jaw dropped as five figures slipped from the darkness, led by a giant red-bearded man. His chest tightened at the first glimpse of violet silk. Perette lifted her skirts and floated down the torchlit path.

"What an enchanting creature." Draven whistled under his breath. "With hair the color of honey."

Raimond stood and shot him a scowl. But when Perette blew a kiss, his face burst back into a smile.

"Surprised, Raimond?" Draven halted the pack at the base of the stage and beckoned their alpha to climb the stairs. "They, along with their odd reversal of an ancient curse, are the decisive reason behind having this trial under a full moon."

"Dogs?" Karl flew into a rage. "What could these filthy beasts possibly add to the proceedings?"

"Character statements," Benjamin said. "And, for the record, they're Wolves of the Loire."

Raimond opened his mouth to speak, but no words came out.

"If only the king were here—"

"But he's not, Karl. I am." Draven nodded his approval and listened to hours of witnesses corroborating Raimond's story. Co-workers from Savannah arrived in droves to extol his virtues as a caregiver and doctor. Lydia crashed down the aisle in her wheelchair, informed the court of her sister Frieda's death, and presented two songbirds from the Blessed Isles as evidence of Raimond's generosity.

Raimond embraced every witness as an honored guest, called them each by name and offered his condolences for those who had passed away. Karl listened until his temper exploded. He kicked his way through the theater wall and stomped into the swamp.

"Is that the last of them?" Draven lurched in his seat. His eyes darted around. "Such riveting testimony, I lost track of time."

"I appreciate your patience, Prince Norman." Raimond stood to keep Benjamin from struggling to his feet. "My defense rests."

"I'll take a few moments to deliberate." Draven stalked down the aisle.

The boy with the broken nose popped up from the last row of seats. "You're scary."

"I wasn't when I was your age." Draven shoved his hands in his pockets. "I am trying to change such perceptions."

"He isn't guilty." The boy pointed to Raimond. "Even a blind man could see that."

Draven regarded the boy and glanced up at his guards. Each man shrugged and nodded. "I believe I'm ready to rule."

Raimond held his arms out. Wolves, nurses and patients gathered around and placed their hands on him in support. Perette wrapped her arms around his chest and buried her face in his shirt. Two tiny glowing birds landed on his shoulder. "We're ready as well."

"So you are. More than anyone I've ever met." The prince climbed the stairs and sat on his throne. "I declare Raimond Banitierre not guilty of treason in the justified death of Faison of Paris."

The courtroom erupted in applause.

"You, sir, have a clean record and are free to leave." Draven paused and retraced his steps across the stage. "You will be the head of your family, with your own sacred book."

Raimond broke the embrace of his friends and sagged to his knees in front of the prince. "Your Highness, I don't know how to—"

"Then don't." Draven motioned for him to stand. "You're officially a survivor and a hero. Many owe thanks to you."

"Faison's book, with my name in it?" Raimond pointed at the old ledger and its black scorpion insignia. "What becomes of that?"

"A dead bloodline." Draven examined crumbling pages. "The only viable names are Parlan Lutaire, and an Anton and Siras. The others have either perished or signed allegiance to another."

"Then those three will receive their own books?" Raimond pressed his palms together.

"Indeed." Draven tossed the ledger in the cauldron. "I assume you know where those individuals are located."

Raimond started to answer and Draven held up a hand to silence him. "Secret royal messengers will deliver them."

The balance in the room shifted as Karl slunk back through the wall's jagged hole.

"You've arrived just in time, Captain." Draven crossed his arms. "To witness the dawn of our new future."

Karl's face remained petrified and unreadable.

"Raimond, I'll soon have a request of my own." Draven gestured to Raimond's mob of friends. "Say your goodbyes. I need to confer with my captain."

Karl bowed his head and waited while Draven scrolled his verdict on official parchment, melted aubergine wax over the cauldron and sealed it with his royal insignia.

"Captain, you may approach." Draven handed him the correspondence. "Deliver this to King Norman."

Karl tucked the document in his breast pocket. "You don't wish to present it yourself?"

"I'll be taking a bit of a side trip." Draven glanced at Raimond. "I have business in Louisiana."

"You can't seriously be considering traveling to…*that* uncivilized destination alone?" Karl growled and gritted his teeth. "Send one of my soldiers to the king. I will accompany you."

"You suffocate me." Draven strutted away. "As if I'm a child," he called over his shoulder.

"Only because you insist on searching for a suitable mate in the land of misfits and lunacy." Karl flashed behind him. "Your Highness, I implore you. It's the most dangerous place on the continent."

"You have your orders." Draven stopped, but didn't turn around. "And mind your own damn business."

Raimond thanked the witnesses, one at a time, and ushered them from the theater.

Perette trembled in the doorway and ran back down the aisle. "I don't want to leave you again, Raimond. Not now, when you need us most."

"*Non, ma petite.*" Raimond pulled a soft handkerchief from his pocket and dried her tears. "You and your brothers deserve to enjoy a full life."

"In the middle of rocks?" Perette sobbed. "I don't understand."

Raimond kissed her on both cheeks. "The Rocky Mountains. The prince says you'll be safe there."

"The range is staggering and breathtaking," Draven spoke from the dark stage. "Miss Perette, I'm confident you'll make a new home there."

"Your bond to me has long been broken." Raimond tipped Perette's chin and locked onto her tear-filled eyes. "What still hurts you so much?"

"This bond will live until I agree to let it go." Perette gulped. "Because…Aveline. If I'd been one second faster, she'd still be alive. I've never repaid that debt to you."

"Shhh, shhh, sweet girl." Raimond crushed her in his arms. "The past has been laid to rest, for all of us."

"How will you find me in these far-away mountains?"

Draven stepped closer. "The instructions I gave to your family send you to a specific town, to a particular man. I'll give Raimond the address."

"Write to me?" Perette leaned back and searched Raimond's face. "*En Francais?*"

"*Oui, mademoiselle.*" Raimond straightened the silk collar of her dress. "Now, you must go."

"I won't forget you, Raimond." Perette linked arms with her brothers on the tattered carpet and took a final glance over her shoulder. "Not ever."

Finally, Raimond folded Benjamin in a long embrace. "You look well, old friend. I can't thank you enough for your assistance."

"It was my pleasure, and not nearly enough to compensate the generosity you've shown us. I'd like to introduce you to someone special." Benjamin looked at Draven, lingering in the shadows. "But your judge seems anxious for us to leave."

"Not at all." Draven approached. "May I meet your lady friend as well?"

"A lady?" Raimond tipped his head. "Is she here?"

Benjamin's outstretched hand was met with delicate fingers and polished nails. "This is my Vera."

"Raimond, you're exactly like my Ben described." Vera's chandelier earrings sparkled as she smiled. "And he talks about you quite a bit."

"Ben, is it?" Raimond winked at him and kissed her hand. "A pleasure to meet you, Miss Vera."

"Intriguing, captivating and fascinating, Miss Vera." Draven introduced himself without his title but bowed with royal grace. "Charmed."

Chapter 23

THE FLOWER GIRL

THE RUINED THEATER'S charged air gradually cleared as each being stepped across the threshold into the murk of the Savannah bayou.

"I would ask you folks to sit, but unfortunately…" Raimond swept his gaze around at the splintered furniture and tossed his hands up. "Tell me, how did you two meet?"

"She's the flower girl," Benjamin whispered.

"I'm the gardener." Vera swatted his shoulder. "Silly man."

"A mystic, a wine lover." Ben held out his arm. "And an expert archer."

Vera linked her elbow with his. "He's the wine connoisseur."

Benjamin met Raimond's wide smile. "She's made me young again."

"She's certainly has." Raimond shook his hand. "You deserve all the happiness in the world."

"We may be feeling our oats," Benjamin sighed, "but staying awake all night is still for the teenagers."

"Good night, Benjamin and Vera." Draven nodded to his soldiers and the double doors creaked open. "I'm positive we'll meet again."

"Be well, Dr. Banitierre." Vera waved before disappearing into the night.

When the room was finally empty, Raimond turned around. "Your Highness, you have a request of me?"

"I do." Draven checked his pocket watch. "Accompany me on a short journey. I'd like to show you something."

"I'm intrigued, but…" Raimond pointed to the gaping hole in the roof and a light grey sky.

"Follow along." Draven swept up the aisle and disappeared into the ruins of the lobby.

Raimond walked backwards to take a final glimpse at the empty theater and lock every detail of the night's proceedings in his mind. *So much to write in my book.* He patted the journal in his secret pocket and paused to memorize carvings on the formerly elegant doors. A grunt from the darkness stopped him in his tracks. "Hello?"

Karl flashed in front of Raimond with his fangs bared.

"May I help you, Captain?"

"You could die. Traitor."

"Not tonight, apparently." Raimond stepped to the side.

"You," Karl puffed out his chest and blocked the way, "have no idea what you're getting into."

"Enlighten me."

"Where to start?" Karl help a finger up for each word. "Fickle, impulsive, damaged."

"I'm sorry you have so many issues." Raimond brushed past him. The scrolled carpet crumbled into dust under his boots.

"Not me, you imbecile. Him!" Karl sprinted around Raimond and pointed outside. "You may be the prince's new favorite, but that never lasts. You'll see."

"I'm sure I can handle it."

"If any harm comes to him in my absence—" Karl grabbed Raimond by the lapels. "I'll hold you responsible and make sure King Norman does too."

Raimond thrust Karl's hands off his jacket and tossed him into a pile of debris. Karl leapt up and both men slammed into the center of the lobby, locked in a standoff.

"Raimond!" From outside, Draven's voice knifed through the tension. "Time is fleeting."

"*Bon nuit*, Captain Karl." Raimond straightened his tie and slipped into the pre-dawn mist.

At the sweeping drive's bend, a carriage waited. Six perfectly matched alabaster horses pranced in place. Raimond climbed into the enormous coach and admired the royal emblems, while Draven chatted with the driver through a sliding panel.

"Are we traveling past the plantation?" Raimond peered through silver-tasseled, velvet drapes. "The one where you arrested me? I left something important there."

Draven knocked on the carriage wall.

The driver's face appeared. "Your Highness?"

"A minor detour to fetch…" Draven looked to Raimond.

"A bottle, or a few bottles." Raimond sat forward. "From under the hearth."

By the time the travelers arrived at the plantation, the eastern horizon was ablaze with light. The human driver followed Raimond's instructions and retrieved the original blood bourbon along with a narrow grey box.

Draven examined the octagonal bottle and raised an eyebrow. "Is it poison?"

"Hardly." Raimond chuckled. "But it is very old."

"Hmm…" Draven removed the cork and sniffed with caution. His eyes glowed bright silver. "May I?"

"Absolutely." Raimond accepted the bottle after Draven sipped, and took a measured swallow. He sat back and groaned in pleasure. "I've tried to replicate it."

Draven flipped open the long box and ran his fingertips over vials swaddled in satin. "Many times, I see. Meticulously labeled."

"Maybe you can detect the ingredient I'm missing." Raimond pulled out the first one.

Draven lifted the bottle to his lips and murmured after tasting each sample. He eventually pointed to a round vial in the middle. "That's the closest in flavor, but there's one glaring issue."

Raimond held his palms up. "I'm listening."

"Magic, or the lack thereof." Draven dabbed the corners of his mouth with a silk pocket square. "The original liquor mixture is heavily spelled with old-world sorcery that should not be underestimated. Was it guarded by griffins?"

"What? No, I found it in the bottom shelf of the damn French clock that captivated your attention." Raimond sat back. His scowl turned into a brief snort and ended as a blank stare. "Griffins?"

"I forget how young you are." Draven ran a hand through his hair. "That timepiece...I've seen it with my own eyes. The Valois threw lavish parties at equally stunning castles and the damn clock was an honored guest at every one."

"Aveline insisted on rescuing the relic. Said it could unlock the future." Raimond pinched the bridge of his nose. "The cost was her precious life."

"I'm shocked anyone found it in one piece. So much history was destroyed."

"The clock was to be a wedding gift for Emily." Raimond slumped lower on the bench as his vision blurred. "I sent for it, from my brother in Scotland."

"We can return to Augusta, slash the throats of everyone involved in the..." Draven's gaze dropped. "I'm sorry about your Emily, truly."

"There's already been so much death." Raimond mumbled, "Too much."

"I've never been engaged, but if someone I loved was murdered." Draven clenched his fist. "I wouldn't be handling it as well as you."

"I'm hopelessly..." Raimond's chest felt like an anvil landed on it. "Mired in the past."

"My father says it's fine to hold onto yesterday, as long as you're forging a passage into tomorrow." Draven swept his arm out with a grand gesture. "Proclaimed it from his throne, so it must be true."

"I feel like this connects me to my history." Raimond cradled the bottle. "There's not much left. When it's gone, it's truly gone."

"Maybe not. Where we're going, you may find some answers."

"Which is where?"

"You'll see." Draven fluffed a pillow and reclined on his bench. "Tell me again, about Faison's tattoos."

Raimond reported every detail he recalled about the living ink and the shapes it took. "Could it have something to do with an actual scorpion?"

"That was more likely the artwork he chose, instead of the donor." Draven reached under the bench, retrieved a flask and took a substantial swallow. "Whiskey?"

"Why not?" Raimond tipped it back.

"The legends of the living ink I referred to were only whispers between the warlocks of my father's court." Draven studied the tufted ceiling. "I may have eavesdropped."

"You?" Raimond handed the flask over with a smirk. "So undignified."

"I was young and quite obsessed with all manner of secrets and dark magic. Supposedly, the ink is blood from deep-sea squids who live their entire lives in pitch blackness, miles from the water's surface."

"How the hell did Faison get that blood?"

"It certainly didn't come free. The only place to find it is the most remote, northern tip of the earth. In a cave of ice, far below the tundra."

"Sounds mythical." Raimond rubbed his eyes. "And slightly impossible. If someone could actually tattoo one of us, wouldn't our bodies just expel the ink?"

"That's where the warlocks come in and why I had to sneak around." Draven rolled on his side to face Raimond. "Another equally important question is: what drove him to make such a perilous journey?"

"He did spout mouthfuls of cryptic nonsense before I ended him …about an eternity of pain and me learning soon enough."

"Classic villain."

"Maybe." Raimond's eyelids grew heavy. "He most likely didn't start out that way." As he spoke, his words drifted off. His eyes opened, closed and fluttered again until they finally stayed shut. His head slumped against the wall. A deep pothole jolted the carriage, sending his face into the window. Raimond bolted up. "You sleep through this?"

Draven chuckled. "Get tired enough, you'll sleep through anything."

The next time Raimond opened his eyes, it was pitch black. The horses were unharnessed and sipping water from a rushing stream, while fires burned around the perimeter of the makeshift camp. Draven sat on a stone bench, smoking a cigar and reading page after silver trimmed page.

That book. Raimond squinted, patted his jacket pocket and found nothing but empty fabric. *My diary!*

"You dropped this item." Draven ignored Raimond's clumsy misstep from the carriage. "It's riveting."

"I beg your pardon? It's blank."

"Brook, a little girl who tragically forgot her own name." Draven flipped back to the first page. "Homeless man in Paris, missing a hand, married his childhood sweetheart. You slit his throat."

"It should be invisible."

"Civil War soldier, Frederick, died the night Sherman burned Atlanta. An accidental overdose. Oh, and the opening line was heart-wrenching…Brothers of the Renegade—"

"Renegade Blood. If you're about to mock us, please don't. It was a long, long time ago."

"Excuse my arrogance, but you'll be brothers of the extinct blood if anyone discovers this."

"The book was spelled." Raimond sat down hard on the bench opposite the prince. "Back in France."

"I'm reading the words. Your words." Draven slammed the cover shut and leaned toward the fire. "Destroy it."

"Those memories are my legacy—" Raimond snatched the journal from his hand. "My salvation."

"If you want to wallow in memories, that's your decision. But you need to keep them up here." Draven tapped his temple. "That little tome could get us all killed. Burn it."

"Giving dignity to the poor, the innocent, the brave…grants meaning to my eternity."

"Rubbish." Draven inhaled sharply through his cigar. "You don't need humans for validation. We're superior in every way."

"More like flawed beyond belief." Raimond pressed the leather cover to his chest and whirled away.

Draven stood and took one step toward the carriage. "Burn it, or I will." He tossed a lighter at Raimond's feet.

Raimond waited until he was alone to pick the lighter out of the grass. He sat on a riverside boulder and cradled his diary.

Finding this in the Augusta rubble was a gift. Maybe the hellfire of a fallen priest could only weaken Aveline's spell, not destroy it.

He rifled through the pages and read snippets of notes.

I remember every detail of these stories. After last night, I'd have so much more to add.

Raimond tossed the book on a flat portion of rock and flicked the lighter open. He took a deep breath and set flame to the red binding. The flare consumed the cover and quickly went out, leaving little damage. Raimond examined the silver lighter's design of scrolls and blue ivy.

Fancy enough.

He flipped the diary over and lit the back cover. Flames barely caught this time and disappeared with no smoke.

More than a little odd.

Raimond peered over his shoulder at the clearing, brimming with royal guards. He gathered a pile of dry sticks and grass from behind the boulder and built a tiny pyre. He flicked the flint mechanism and adjusted the flame to maximum height before touching the kindling.

That should do it.

Black smoke still wafted from the river's edge as Raimond returned to the carriage. He discovered several more coaches parked behind it. The impatient snorts of horses and jingling harnesses echoed across the valley.

"I nearly came after you." Draven leaned out the window. "We have a schedule to keep."

Raimond climbed in and settled onto his bench. "This is quite an entourage."

"Always is when I travel." Draven wrestled a cloth from the overhead bin. "Did you take a bath?"

"Merci." Raimond tousled his damp hair and dried his face. "Just rinsed the soot off."

Draven knocked on the front wall and the carriage wheels rolled. "One more stop, and then straight through to our destination."

Raimond nodded and settled into the sea of cushions and blankets on his luxurious bunk. Every few minutes his hand wandered to his securely buttoned trouser pocket and took comfort at the edges of his journal. *The book that wouldn't burn.*

Chapter 24

RENEGADE BLOOD

THE ROYAL CAVALCADE split on the outskirts of a small village. Raimond bolted up at the sudden change in direction. Through the windows he watched sparse huts merge with modest brick houses, until they reached the immaculate town center. The scrolled signs and shingles along main street advertised all the day-to-day necessities, along with high class services and merchandise.

"No worries." Draven reclined on his velvet bench. "Established security protocols."

"I hope we're here to feed."

"Indeed." Draven rubbed his palms together. "Feeling the glorious urge to bite someone?"

Raimond's head fell into his hands. "I sense I'm being corrupted."

"You're welcome." Draven leapt from the carriage the moment it stopped at a tavern. "This establishment has the tastiest barmaids."

"Captain Karl mentioned you were searching for a mate."

"Not here." Draven scoffed. "I have exacting standards."

"Of course, you do." Raimond ducked through the entrance to see two young women rushing to the prince's side. He nearly backed out the door before their pulses assaulted his ears and wrenched him forward. "Bloody hell, I need to drink more often."

"You need proof I'm not an indiscriminate killer?" Draven leaned on the bar and held out both hands. One woman wiggled into his arms while the other placed a frothy drink in his palm. "I may be a house favorite."

"Whenever the blond gentleman is in town," the woman in his arms kissed his cheek, "we have the grandest time."

"Is it a brothel?" Raimond sighed and shuffled closer. "Or a bar?"

"Strictly the latter, for tonight." Draven squeezed the barmaid's waist. "Darling, stand the doctor a proper drink."

"Ooo, a doctor?" She pulled another beer and winked. "I could use a good going-over."

Draven motioned Raimond toward a dark corner, away from rowdy patrons. "You see I've not alarmed or injured the ladies in any way."

"And they do seem fond of you."

"Go ahead and feed from one, or both." Draven sipped his drink, spit it back in the glass and searched for the flask in his pocket. "The blood is considerably better than this swill."

Raimond shook his head.

"Forge on, chin up. When you're finished, plant an absurdly scandalous story in everyone's pretty mind." A twirl of his fingers summoned the bustier of the two, who winked and crooked her finger before disappearing into the back room. "I'll be waiting."

Raimond ran his fingers over the stubble on his chin and straightened his collar before stepping into the bar. "Your Highness, you were right, I—"

The previously crowded tavern was silent and empty, except for one table draped by damask linen and set with crystal far too fancy for everyday use. Benjamin looked over with a friendly wave.

"Raimond." Draven sprung up. "Nothing is wrong."

"Benjamin, has there been an accident?" Raimond ran to the vacated chair. "Vera, are you hurt?"

"No, son, we're here to help." Benjamin patted his hand.

"Draven." Raimond ground his teeth. "What. Is. This?"

"An intervention." Draven placed both his hands flat, on the tablecloth. "For both sides."

Raimond's blank stare shot from face to face to face, before straying to the front door.

"No, Raimond." Vera clung to his sleeve. "Don't run. This is about our safety as well."

"We know certain…secrets." Benjamin sighed at Draven. "Your judge offered us protection, along with an intriguing proposal."

"It's imperative that you have an inner circle." Draven stood straight. "These two aren't young on paper, but—"

"But good Lord." Vera rolled her eyes. "We're in better shape than most."

"Thanks to Vera's potions." Benjamin flexed his biceps.

"You must be insane," Raimond hissed. "Every one of you."

"We want to be like you, Raimond," Benjamin said. "There's so much going on in the world—"

"We don't want to miss out on the future." Vera pressed her palms together. "We'll never be younger than we are today."

"You have no idea…" Raimond clawed his hands across his face. "What you're asking. No inkling."

"We do, actually." Vera retrieved a tattered, barely bound manuscript from her purse and placed it on the table.

"It's her grimoire." Benjamin flipped it open to a ragged, dog-eared page and pointed to the chapter title.

"Aveline had a grimoire." Raimond examined the fancy lettering and glared at Draven. "Blood Drinkers?"

"Heavens." Draven clasped his hands behind his back. "Raimond, you must comprehend that they know too much."

"They could be made to forget," Raimond sniped. "The safest option."

"Unacceptable. My mind is finally clear." Benjamin pounded his fist on the table. "We do not wish to forget—not you—not anything!"

Draven tapped his foot. "Founding members of your new family?"

"I've never." Raimond leapt up and crumpled into the bar. "I can't imagine."

"I'll help you." Draven hauled him upright. "My inspiration, your blood."

"I need to think it over." Raimond paced the floor. *The point of no return.*

"Do you?" Draven nodded to Benjamin and Vera. Their faces lit up like teenagers in love. "Do you, really?"

"I need a minute." Raimond stormed outside and screamed so loud, it shook the leaves off the trees.

Draven waited in the doorway until the forest plunged back into silence and Raimond returned. "You're confident of the procedure?"

"No." Raimond jumped back and squeezed his head. "I've read instructions in Aveline's pretty handwriting. She drew kittens in the margin."

"Not precisely the mood for this event." Draven swept his hand out. "Turn the gentleman first. Learn from your mistakes."

"You're aware I'm a doctor?" Raimond stormed away. "I don't tolerate mistakes."

Draven wobbled his head and ushered Vera to the backroom. "Ladies, talk amongst yourselves."

"I need to be with my Ben." Vera tried to dodge around Draven.

"Miss Vera." Draven intercepted her and bent down to meet her eyes. "The plan is for you two to be together forever, but Raimond requires time alone with your beau."

"Just a few minutes, then." Vera nodded sluggishly. "What should we talk about?"

"Well." Draven motioned to the two barmaids. "Whatever women talk about when men aren't around. Face powder, flowers, chipmunks?"

"Oh, my goodness." The barmaid yanked wine from a cupboard and took Vera's hand. "We talk about men, and how daft you idiots can be."

Draven spun around after the door slammed in his face.

Raimond snickered. "But they were so fond of you."

"I'm sure they meant someone else less…refined." Draven looked back and forth between Raimond and Benjamin. "All set?"

"I'm completely against this entire—" Raimond groaned at Benjamin's pleading gaze. "I know how you love Christmas dinner. Are you prepared to give all that up?"

"I'll be a hero to every pig and turkey on earth." Benjamin placed his hand over his heart. "My decision is final."

"Remember the progression." Draven flashed his fangs.

"Yes, kill the poor human, force blood down their throat and squeeze the heart?"

"Try some artistry, some elegance. Extinguish, replenish, resuscitate…" He flared his fingers and tiny sparks lit the dark bar. "Ignite."

Benjamin stood, faced Draven and squared his shoulders. "I assume this will hurt."

"No more than a mosquito bite." Draven scrolled a curvy line in the air. Benjamin's eyes reflected his motion and glazed over. "Stop pacing, Raimond. He's numb."

Raimond froze behind Benjamin. "That's possible?"

"It is for me." Draven rubbed his chin. "Royalty can be a dreadful burden, but it does have perks. You'll need to hurry."

Raimond tipped Benjamin's head to the side and loosened his collar. "This violates every ounce of soul I have left."

"I don't envy your position." Draven ripped open Benjamin's shirt. "Bite him, now. Suck hard and don't stop until I give you permission."

Raimond pounded his forehead with his fist before driving his fangs into Benjamin's neck. Blood that burned his throat like acid in the first swallows, sweetened like an explosion of sugar as he absorbed his friend's cherished memories and history of brave love.

"Don't stop…a few more heartbeats." Draven forced Benjamin's flesh into Raimond's fangs. "Stop!"

Raimond glanced up at his reflection in a grimy mirror. *I don't even recognize myself.* Benjamin's full weight landed in his arms. He struggled to work his wrist free. "Should I replenish?"

"Rip an artery open." Draven repositioned Raimond's forearm.

Raimond tore at his own flesh until blood oozed out. He forced black liquid down Benjamin's throat. "What now?"

"Resuscitate. Circulate your venom." Draven pointed at the man's chest. "Plunge your hand in!"

"This is barbaric." Raimond gagged and slammed through Benjamin's flesh, bone and vessels before wavering and drooping to the floor.

"Stop fiddling around." Draven grabbed Raimond's blank face. "Your dear friend has an expiration time, when he will be...just hopelessly, miserably dead."

"Squeeze his heart?" Raimond choked back tears.

"Gently." Draven held up his palm and rippled his fingers. "Tenderly."

Raimond massaged Benjamin's heart until Draven placed an ice-cold hand on his arm. "Is it enough?"

"Plenty." Draven hoisted Benjamin's body into a chair. "There's one more step."

Raimond slumped next to the dead man. "Ignite?"

"Seven drops is the minimum." Draven snapped his fingers and the barmaid emerged from the back room. He cooed at the woman, ripped her wrist open and squeezed bright red blood down Benjamin's throat. "More is generally better."

Raimond dropped his forehead to the table. "It's finally over?"

"For him, you big baby." Draven picked Raimond's skull up with a handful of hair. "Vera is next. Try not to be so sloppy."

Chapter 25

FORTRESS OF RUIN

THE HORSE DRAWN carriage clattered to a stop on a sloppy road atop the Mississippi River levee. The driver waited for the sun to slip below the horizon before opening the elegantly draped back door.

"Raimond!" Draven adjusted his top hat and stepped out. "We've arrived."

"Arrived where, exactly?" Raimond gripped the door frame and stumbled out of the carriage. "How do you look so dapper after being jostled across the countryside?"

"You'll learn, in time." Draven flung open his arms and embraced the darkness. "So, your opinion?"

Raimond's eyes wandered to the muddy river, across the desolate road and then up a gentle hill to the outline of a structure. He blinked and refocused. The dark, glowing green of the lawn struck him first and then vibrant, tropical colors assaulted him from every direction. "My opinion on what?"

"Your new home, of course." Draven forged up the slope. "You'll need to use some creative ingenuity."

"I'm not sure I'm ready for—" Raimond hung back. "You are aware of what happened to my last home?"

"What are the odds of that happening again?" Draven waved him forward. "Trust me, this is a hidden gem and your life is about to change."

The pair approached the mansion, or what was left of it. A double staircase that had swept to the right and left in its younger days, sagged in ruin. Raimond leapt onto the wide veranda, dodged holes in the wooden planks and peered through warped front doors.

"I've employed a family of caretakers and paid them excessively well. They officially own the property." Draven boldly stepped across the threshold. "DeLynch! Where are you, good man?"

A butler wearing a flawless livery emerged from the rear of the mansion, carrying a modern gas lamp.

"Your Highness?" He brushed nonexistent dust off his lapels. "Sir?"

"DeLynch." Draven swept out his hand. "My newest associate and future head of this estate, Dr. Raimond Banitierre."

"Welcome, welcome." DeLynch ushered him into the crumbling foyer. "Our glorious house is in dire need of help."

"Indeed, it is." Raimond pulled vines from the marble bannister that disappeared into the collapsed upper floor. "Draven, you must have a motive for showing me this disaster. I'm a soldier and a doctor, not an architect or designer."

"Well, I'm always available to assist with furniture choices." Draven read Raimond's confused look. "An estate like this, restored to her former glory, is a critical puzzle piece."

DeLynch shuffled across the tiles and forced open carved doors. "Dr. Banitierre, this room was the jewel of the house, once upon a time."

"And this?" Raimond lifted the corner of an old sheet up to see a heap of colored glass.

"Our grand skylight." DeLynch fought back a tear.

Raimond knelt and rubbed soot off the floor to reveal gleaming white wood. "Critical for what, Draven?"

"I'd like to name the mansion Normandie Hall." Draven drifted into moonlight streaming through the hole where the skylight belonged. "And I'd like to gift it to you as the official residence of my newly appointed Duke."

"Your Highness." Raimond stayed kneeling and bowed his head. "Words can't express how grateful I am that you found me not guilty, but what qualifies me to be royalty? I'm a common peasant."

Draven leaned forward. "That humility, along with your natural leadership is what makes you the perfect candidate for the job. New Orleans has fallen into disarray and I don't have the desire or patience to control that irreverence."

"New Orleans?" Raimond kept his head bowed. "I've only heard stories."

"All lies." Draven chuckled. "The truth is far more sordid."

The evening hush was broken only by the pounding of the mighty Mississippi and the harmony of the deep swamp, until DeLynch's knee thudded onto the floor. "I'll be forever at your service, my Duke."

Raimond shook his head and raised his eyes to meet Draven's. "Are you absolutely certain?"

"Beyond a doubt," Draven answered. "The only remaining decision is your title. Orleans or Normandie perhaps?"

"Those names have been used and abused back in France. I'd insist on keeping Banitierre. My family deserves at least that much recognition."

"Granted." Draven unsheathed a jeweled dagger and laid it on Raimond's shoulder. "I bless you with the title Duke Raimond of the Royal House Banitierre." He lifted and twirled the blade to rest on Raimond's other shoulder. "I grant you the fortress, Normandie Hall and stewardship of the great city of New Orleans."

"Will this be official enough?" Raimond asked. "To satisfy your other subjects, I mean."

"We'll do it again, in front of everyone who matters," Draven said. "But I've decided. Fools who stand against the Normans are dead fools."

"Thank you, Your Highness." Raimond kissed the Prince's ring and gazed around at the decaying walls. "Where do I even start rebuilding?"

"I'm sure DeLynch will be a tremendous help filling in the historical details." Draven motioned for the butler to stand.

"I will Your Highness," DeLynch murmured. "With the greatest pleasure."

"What about Benjamin and Vera?" Raimond peered back at the convoy of carriages.

"Already safely in the basement." Draven waved off Raimond's puzzled stare. "The house has an extensive subterranean complex."

"If you say so."

"I promise it's secure and not a dungeon." Draven peeked into the rear parlor and then into its twin overlooking the river. "Where's the French clock again?"

"As far as I know, the Port of Savannah."

"You should place it here, between the parlors." Draven pointed at a cracked wall. "In honor of your beloved Emily."

Raimond kicked debris away and surveyed an empty space in the foyer. "It would certainly fit."

"Before you launch into all that." Draven motioned to the door. "We have one more destination on this trip. I saved the best for last."

"Is there drinking involved, because I'm feeling—" Raimond leaned on the peeling white wall for balance.

"Piqued?" Draven swept across the veranda and jumped to the wet lawn. "The hunger rolls off you in waves."

Raimond nodded to DeLynch and followed the prince. The long blast of a riverboat whistle pierced heavy air.

"That right there," Draven pointed to the paddle-wheeler, lit up like a floating carnival, "is our chariot to the greatest hunting grounds in the world."

"Just one minute." Raimond grabbed an octagonal bottle from the inside corner of the carriage and dashed back to the dark mansion. He found the butler sitting on the crumbling stairs. "I have a favor to ask."

"Sir!" De Lynch bolted up. "At your service, sir."

"This bottle is a special blend of bourbon and blood, rescued from a royal French cellar." Raimond held out the glass container. "Any chance you can replicate it, or know someone who might help?"

"Any hints on the list of ingredients?"

"I'm told the original creators were witches. There may or may not have been griffins—" Raimond pinched the bridge of his nose. "Or dragon-like creatures involved."

"Most likely." De Lynch nodded. "We have superb local resources. Surely, they will uncover the correct recipe."

Raimond gazed around the house and scratched his chin. His attention lingered on the gap left by an absent chandelier, voids where gas lamps had lit hallways, and the overgrown garden creeping through shattered French doors. "Right here!" He shuffled to the curved wall under the grand staircase and extended his arms to measure the space. "This is where we'll put the Christmas tree."

DeLynch tipped his head.

"The biggest one, I mean." Raimond energetically brushed away dust and rubble. "Every room will have its own with a unique theme. Can't you just see the glitter, smell the evergreen boughs and hear the carols?"

The butler's face exploded in a smile. "It is that blessed time of year."

Raimond gazed through the hole in the roof at a foggy night sky. "I miss my birds."

"We have the facilities to keep falcons if you like?"

"Mine were a bit smaller." Raimond smiled. "Until I return then, DeLynch?"

"I anxiously await your residence." DeLynch dropped his eyes and bowed. "Honored Duke Banitierre."

Raimond jogged to the riverboat and bowed to the Prince. "*Je suis désolé,* Your Highness. Now, where are the greatest hunting grounds on our blessed earth?"

"For someone who hates France, you still speak a fair bit of French."

"It seems to charm the ladies."

"Well, that particular language may serve you well where we're going." The prince marched down the gangplank. The crew tossed lines and the ship powered away from the river bank, while the prince leaned his face back to bask in sultry moonlight. "Tomorrow night I'll take you on the grand tour and introduce a staggering cast of characters before inducting you as vampire royalty."

"Allies?"

"A few. Many selfish agendas and idiotic chaos as well." Draven plucked a cigar from his pocket. "I'll lend you some soldiers until you establish your own force."

Raimond glanced around at royal guards stationed along the rails and nodded. "A decent start."

"Not nearly enough." Draven faced the river, raised his fist to the darkness and whistled.

Like a chain of stars being born, torches illuminated the levee and river bank as far as Raimond could see.

"Fit for a commander?"

"Larger than any army I've ever had." Raimond took a moment to collect his thoughts. "Seems an odd time to ask, but is there any chance I can resurrect my medical career?"

"Quite possibly." Draven waved a flame under the tip of his cigar. "The Sisters of the Peace are expanding their dingy hospital and incessantly begging for help. Please make them stop."

"I'll do my best." Raimond leaned on the railing and followed the moon's silver trail on the water. "So, I begin again."

Chapter 26

EVENING CALL

THE YELP OF a single dog triggered the whinny of a horse, expletives shouted in a world of accents, a thunderous crash and an explosion of howling.

"Is it always so noisy on these docks?" Raimond straightened his tie, wiped steam from the gangway mirror and combed his hair back. He tousled it again and tossed up his hands. "So incessantly loud?"

"Machinery and animals work around the clock." Draven smoothed his lapels. "And we've tied up downriver of the busiest wharfs."

The whoosh and hiss of a steam engine firing up nearby was followed by a moaning whistle that grew into a rollicking melody.

"Cheerful as it is, that calliope is deafening. I've no idea what to expect when the sun goes down."

"No, my friend, you do not. This is the Vieux Carré." Draven peeked through brocade curtains. "A few more moments."

Raimond shifted his gaze. "You're certain I'll like it?"

"The most preposterous question ever asked." Draven burst onto deck in the first seconds of dusk. "You're wasting precious time, Duke."

Royal security, along with meticulously selected local law enforcement, led the procession.

Raimond wasn't fazed when a wharf full of workers and wagons silently parted, allowing them to pass. He didn't notice the din of the calliope fade or the earth's tremor as he stepped across quivering steel railroad tracks. Before the entourage reached the busy street, he glimpsed three spires piercing a crimson and purple sky, and finally froze. "Must go there."

"Patience, please. The cathedral is on my royal tour." Draven pointed up and down a busy street. "Rue de La Leveé."

"Sign says Decatur."

"I'm resistant to change." Draven motioned for him to follow.

Raimond took one step forward and swayed. "But that intoxicating smell."

"You've never tasted anything like the blood in this—"

"I meant the coffee." Raimond wandered left, to a long low building and stopped in front of a shop at the very end.

Draven sighed and backtracked. "I do anticipate an eventful night." He led the way under an arched sign, leaned on the glossy counter and glanced at the guards behind him. They were dressed down yet not blending well into the crowd. He handed the waiter a stack of silver coins.

"Sir, this is far too much."

"A cup for each of my friends, black. Also, a complimentary beverage for every patron in your establishment. No change necessary."

Scowls and frowns from the locals changed into handshakes and shared cigarettes.

"I can be generous." Draven turned to smirk at Raimond over his first sip of coffee. "To advance my own agenda."

"I know this wasn't the first planned stop on your itinerary." Raimond slumped against a white column and savored his coffee. "But it's delicious." He nodded at a brick building on the next corner. "What manner of house is that?"

"The home of money. Gold and silver…they mint it, in case you're ever in need of cash. Now, this is quite the tasty brew, but our dazzling Crescent City awaits." Draven summoned the Royal Guard's newly promoted senior officer. "I'm sure you know how Captain Karl would handle this situation?"

"Of course." The soldier bowed.

"Do the exact opposite." Draven handed him the coffee cup. "We're here for a stroll, not an invasion."

"Yes, Your Highness." The guard juggled empty china. "A discreet distance."

"One more thing, soldier." Draven exchanged glances with Raimond and pointed to a tall guard. "I don't know him."

"That human?" The senior officer snapped to attention. "He's Ronald. A highly qualified citizen expert."

"Recommended by whom?"

"The Roussels, Your Highness." The soldier dropped his eyes. "But if you'd like me to dismiss him—"

"No, having a mortal on the team is progressive and invaluable. Tall Ronald stays." Draven turned to Raimond and lowered his voice. "A word of advice. Pay close attention to everything you see, smell, hear and touch in this city—all the firsts. It's not just unique architecture and pretty harmony, but threads of wisdom woven into your tapestry of power."

"Understood." Raimond straightened his shoulders.

Draven glanced around. "Gentlemen, shall we?"

Raimond drained his coffee cup, tried to mimic Draven's swagger across Decatur Street and nearly fell in the gutter.

"Careful, the footing is often deceptive. Now, this building," Draven pointed to a dormered three-story structure that commanded two city blocks. He made a sharp right turn and stopped to gaze through an iron gate. "Used to be full of nuns."

"And now?"

"They built a newer, bigger convent...blocks...over there." Draven waved a hand behind his head, scanned the street and leaned closer. "Rumor has it, they still own a piece of every property in town."

"Pristine gardens."

"The Archbishop currently lives here." Draven dove out of sight. "And not all the devout sisters have left."

Raimond peered around the edge of the stone wall. "I've never seen a nun wear a habit that color before. It flows behind her like the train of a wedding dress."

"Sapphire is the color of power here." Draven hauled him across the street. "Most holy women don't like our kind."

"Most? But some do?" Raimond shadowed Draven around two left turns. They stopped in front of ornate gates and peeked down narrow alleys. Brilliant specks of blue peeked out everywhere. "I'll need further explanation."

"Tour now, stories later." Draven slowed in front of a lavish home to let his friend catch up. "If you ever build a house, employ this architect."

Raimond's gaze wandered over the granite façade and up to green metal iron arches that crowned the gallery. "Very unique."

"I've been invited in several times." Draven pointed through the covered carriageway. "Indoor plumbing and ventilation. The designer, Gallier, is a genius ahead of his time."

"And these patterns?" Raimond touched the scrolled gate.

"By the same man. I believe that is cast iron." Draven drove his hands into his pockets and sauntered to the center of Rue Royale's cobblestones. "But if you fancy wrought iron, you've arrived in heaven."

Raimond joined him, and a tunnel of lace iron unfolded as far as he could see. He followed as the prince took the lead again, pointing out houses and rattling off an endless list of French names. He nearly collided with Draven at the next corner.

"This is a private home as well?" Raimond craned his neck to see the third story gallery, draped with flowers.

"The townhouse of a founding Creole family."

Raimond was drawn to an arched doorway. "They must have running water."

"That's a fountain." Draven rolled his eyes and nodded down the dim hall. "In the courtyard."

"Can you imagine living in a home like this?" Raimond focused on the tiered sculpture in the center of a glowing oasis. "Well, of course you can."

"You too will get your palace, Duke." Draven rubbed his chin. "This place does look more like a hotel. Someday, it may be one."

"The fountain feature must be common."

Draven raised an eyebrow.

"I hear so many…" Raimond rubbed his ears. "Hundreds. Sounds like a waterfall on top of a brass band."

"I think we need a short break from sightseeing, before you're completely flabbergasted."

"I'm not overwhelmed—but the music is so clear. Like it's coming from nowhere and everywhere at once." Raimond wandered down a side street until Draven's guards appeared and steered him back. "Wait, isn't that…"

"The famous Rue Bourbon, yes. We'll visit later, just not this particular block."

"Across the street…is that wheat?" Raimond stopped and blinked hard. "Forged from metal?"

"Cornstalks, actually." Draven hurried him toward a single doorway in a long brick wall. "There's some touching story which I don't recall at the moment."

Once Raimond ducked through the ivy-draped gate, his ears were bombarded with the sound of silverware clinking against china. He followed Draven out to a courtyard while guards gave orders to the host.

"Our private suite will be ready in a few moments." Draven casually leaned on the bar and perused the liquor collection.

"They have private rooms?"

"Every establishment does, though most keep them secret." Draven shrugged off his jacket and handed it to an attendant, motioning for Raimond to do the same. "I know you have a million questions, but can you tolerate Absinthe?"

"A splash."

"Splendid." Draven caught the bartender's eye. "Two Sazeracs."

"First question." Raimond removed the curled lemon garnish before sniffing his drink. "What's wrong with that particular block of Bourbon?"

Draven retrieved the discarded lemon and dropped it in his glass. "Pirates."

"I'm sure that's a riveting tale." Raimond tipped his head and drained the tumbler. "Another, *s'il vous plaît*."

"Your reservation is ready." A waiter in an immaculate tuxedo swept out his hand.

Raimond sipped his second drink, admiring greenery and flowers sculpted around the courtyard. Each square featured a small fountain or cluster of candles in the center. He quickened his step to keep pace with Draven.

The waiter led the way through a maze of gates and portals, into a staircase. Each step creaked with a unique voice as they worked their way up.

At the first landing, Draven pointed to a dimly lit hall. "Cypress dining table."

Raimond stepped in and ran his fingers over the satin finish of an eight-pointed rose compass. "Brilliant inlay work."

"The artisan who crafted that only made three pieces. You'll see another later tonight."

"And the third?" Raimond glanced back.

"That third one was actually the artist's first creation. It's been missing since the fire of 1794," Draven answered. "Some say it was saved by those sapphire nuns, but it's definitely not in the convent anymore."

The climb ended in a third-floor library. Stained glass sconces and dark paneling lent the room a lush and eerie glow. Draven selected a cigar from a silver tray and toasted it in the long match lit by the waiter. The room's balcony featured a view through the mismatched buildings, all the way to the river.

"You're welcome to smoke as well." Draven puffed rings over his head.

Raimond rummaged through his pocket and unwrapped a foil package containing a brown cigarette. "I've only got one of these favorites left."

"Ah, cloves." Draven handed him a box of matches. "You can buy those many places in town, but one source stocks only the best. It's also on our tour."

Raimond inhaled and let his eyes drift closed.

"Any regrets yet, Duke?"

"About the view? Or blunders of my past?"

"About anything. I'm all ears." Draven leaned on the burnished railing. "But no wallowing in guilt."

"To be honest, I've always dreamed of becoming a father. That fantasy has hit a snag."

"Not as seriously as you think. You'll have plenty of family drama here…no need to be a biblical father." Draven tapped his ashes in a marble dish and smirked. "Why do you think I'm stepping away?"

Surrounded by wisps of smoke, both men fell silent and allowed the city's sacred vibrance to find her voice. Raimond's attention was stolen again by three spires visible over the roofline. On the highest peak, a cross glowed in the lingering twilight.

"That is truly magnificent." Raimond squinted into the dark. "I almost saw…a lady with wings, dancing along the spine of the roof."

"Well, there's a painting on the ceiling that's rumored to be a window to heaven. We're on our way there, no worries." Draven snuffed his cigar and ducked through the balcony doors. "First, some sustenance."

Raimond found strangers waiting inside, sipping wine and staring into space with glassy eyes. Human heartbeats, slightly muted by the cloves, drummed in his ears.

"Merely an appetizer." Draven tossed off his tie and slid onto the plush sofa next to a blonde lady. He trailed kisses from her hand, bared his fangs and zeroed in on her neck.

Chapter 27

RAGING GIANTS

"THAT WAS A bit more indulgent that an appetizer." Raimond wiped a drop of blood from his chin and tossed his stained tie on a mahogany end table. He lingered to watch the guards take final sips of the leftovers and embed stories in the human's minds.

Draven stopped on the first landing and peered up. "What did I tell you about the blood here?"

"I may never get enough." Raimond hustled to catch up, stopped to glance at the courtyard and walked cautiously down two more flights searching for the prince. "I'm pleased that all the donors survived."

"What do you think I am, a barbarian?" Draven struck a match, lit a fat candle and continued his descent. "On second thought, don't answer that." He touched the candle to a torch on the wall, igniting a trail of blazing beacons down a tunnel.

Raimond's jaw dropped. "Looks like it goes on forever."

"There used to be a network under the entire Quarter. Now, it's only this corridor and a solitary room a few blocks away."

Raimond covered both his ears and swallowed hard. "That jarring pressure…is it the river?"

"Takes a lot of magic to hold even this short portion of the passage open. Much as I love it down here, your resources would be better spent on an elite security force." Draven sighed and ran his finger along the dripping wall. "Shall we walk?"

Raimond glanced up at the sliver of light from the courtyard and flashed into the menacing darkness. Magic spit them out in a shrouded ballroom with dark chandeliers and the most ornate medallions he had ever seen. An old nun in a blue habit made the sign of the cross over her chest before clicking the door shut with both vampires safely hidden inside.

"Don't worry. She won't talk." Draven walked up three steps, cast open tall doors and stepped onto the gallery. "And if you want to know the secrets of that room, the government conspiracies, presidential announcements or quadroon balls, ask me. I've witnessed every moment."

In a blur of supernatural speed, the prince leapt from the gallery onto Rue D'Orleans. He stood stone still until Raimond landed at his side.

No one in the vicinity noticed their intrusion, no one even missed a step until Raimond stumbled at the back gate of St. Louis Cathedral. He pulled himself upright with the fence. The moment his skin touched the iron bars, candles flickering around the base of a white statue blazed with vigor. The figure reflected on the cathedral's back wall transformed from a sacred symbol into a raging giant.

"There's a new twist." Draven's eyes widened as Raimond let go of the fence and the reflection melted away. "Which did not go unnoticed. Let's keep moving."

Security guards fanned out with precision, greeting each perplexed human and erasing their memory of the strange fire. Ronald walked behind, making sure every person had resumed their routines. After damage control was complete, the guards assisted in keeping Raimond walking forward although he stopped in front of every window, mesmerized, as if he had never seen luxury items before.

A sharp right onto Rue Toulouse broke Raimond's trance. "Did you see the jeweled tones of those lamps and chandeliers? I need to go back to that shop."

"I recall you declaring that you weren't much of a decorator. Plenty of time for browsing later." Draven halted at the corner and pointed to the sign.

"Rue Bourbon." Raimond followed Draven's gaze across the street. *"Mon dieu."*

"Most likely, God will not join us at the French Opera House. But we'll attend a performance in my private box before leaving town."

Raimond's jaw dropped as his eyes traveled up the soaring colonnades.

"Also designed by James Gallier, the architect I recommended earlier. A grand elliptical hall, four tiers of seats, all adorned in white and dazzling red."

"Sounds spectacular."

"And the ladies that attend these events." Draven kissed his fingers. "An endless buffet of exotic blood. I hope we don't quarrel over the same woman."

"I'm just a humble doctor, with simple tastes."

"We shall see." Draven strutted across the street. "The theater is dark tonight, but come, peek through the curtains."

Raimond cupped his hand to the sparkling glass and let out a low whistle. "They must be rehearsing."

"For the United States premiere of Salammbô, I'm sure. Opening night promises to be—"

"Controversial?"

"Magnificently so, and this city will embrace it."

"Those chandeliers." Raimond slid to a taller window for a better view of the lobby's grand staircase. "Every time the auditorium door cracks open, just that sliver of glow wakes a rainbow."

"Garden sheds are lit with crystal around here. Move along." Draven whipped out his pocket watch and groaned. "We've got a list of clubs to visit. Did you ever attend the Moulin Rouge?"

"Unfortunately, not as a patron, although the streets around it and Montmartre were lucrative hunting grounds."

"Then you're in for a treat tonight. We'll hit the highlights."

"I'll admit," Raimond turned in a circle, "it's not as seedy as I expected."

"The real debauchery resides a few short blocks back, in the vice district." Draven headed away from the river. "I'll show you a safe place to indulge in sinful desires you don't even know you possess. There's a menu-book of sorts, so you can pick and choose the perfect woman or two. Maybe three."

"Sounds degrading."

"Treat them like princesses, leave a staggering tip." Draven patted a pocket of jingling coins. "You'll be a house favorite, swimming in fine champagne."

Raimond stopped to peek through the doors of each burlesque club. Each bar offered a different style of music. Refined old world standards blended with raucous improvisation and Caribbean flair. Dancers adorned in fringe and tassels implored him to enter.

"If you absolutely must," Draven grimaced, "you may steal energy from any human at these venues."

"I prefer the term sample."

"Of course you do, and it's not even pretentious when you say it."

"I'll take that as a compliment." Raimond drew a deep breath. "The lifeforce here is amazing. People mingling— vibrant and alive, yet ancient and wise. I've drawn strength from so many citizens already whose New Orleans roots go back generations. The cultures are diverse and fascinating, especially in the older souls." Raimond chased Draven across Rampart Street as he ventured farther from the river. "I notice you've taken nothing."

"I'm royalty, I don't need it. Very little about human essence impresses me and most definitely not the elderly. Their lives are over." Finally, the prince stood motionless below a scarlet sign on the corner of Basin Street. The stairs of the building led to black doors, guarded by two enormous men.

"It's the least glitzy place on the block. This is your favorite?"

"You'll soon see why." Draven nodded and guards threw open the doors. In the front, where a hostess would normally sit, a woman stood on the desk. Dressed in a top hat, fishnet stockings, high black boots and very little else, she crossed her arms and glared down at the men.

"Mr. Norman." A smile hooked the corner of her mouth. "Please, do come in."

The men settled into the serpentine bend of a glowing cherry bar. Hundreds of electric lights twinkled under a polished tin ceiling. Drinks were served immediately and dancers emerged from the stage wings, beseeching them to watch with seductive gestures, feathers and fans.

"At all the other places we've visited, you may only absorb energy. But here you should drink like the ultimate demon that you are." Draven kissed the hand of a girl with a flawless olive complexion as she led him toward the private rooms. "My dear, you are ravishing tonight. I love it when you wear the gifts I bring." Dangling from the jeweled chain around her waist, a diamond pendant swayed just below her navel. "Raimond, indulge until you're satiated. Just remember, the night is very young."

Draven returned to the bar to find Raimond deep in conversation with the club's owner. With fascination, he watched the doctor examine one of her crooked fingers, reset the bone and immediately erase any memory of discomfort. He expertly fashioned a splint out of wood and strips of linen.

"At least let me pay you, Doctor." The woman set aside her jewel encrusted cigarette holder and rummaged through the cash register.

"I won't hear of it." Raimond shook his head until she clicked the brass register's drawer shut. "That lovely smile is all the reward I need."

"He will let you buy both of us a drink, though." Draven settled on a bar stool. "Did you find companionship?"

Raimond nodded to the woman. "Miss Cleo was in tremendous pain."

"More tedious names?" Draven pounded his fist into his forehead. "Raimond, I said anonymous, fast and tidy."

"No, you didn't and you should hear the stories our hostess has told me, about the town and how she and her husband opened this club."

"God rest his soul." Cleo delivered two double bourbons and flipped open a long cigar box. A southern lady in a stylish hat adorned the painted lid.

"Fascinating history." Raimond declined the cigars, sipped bourbon and hummed his approval. "The piano player's talent is riveting."

"Our resident professor." Cleo gestured toward a glossy white grand piano. "Shall I introduce you?"

"Later, Cleo. Our night still has a loaded agenda." Draven snapped his fingers at a shadowy figure in the corner and lifted the tumbler from Raimond's hand. "I'll safeguard the liquor. You will sample a perfectly exquisite, favorite flavor of mine. Melody, come out here, precious."

Raimond stood and waited while a barefoot girl emerged from the shrouded back lounge. "*Enchanté, mademoiselle.*"

"So polite." She giggled when Raimond's lips brushed the silky bronze skin of her hand, trailing kisses past an array of jeweled bracelets and up her slender wrist. "Melody isn't my real name."

"I'm fairly certain it's not Precious, either." Raimond fitted his arm around her waist and worked his deep gaze past her feathery lashes. "Miss Kimberly, I'm happy to make your acquaintance. One moment, *s'il vous plait.* I worry about my friend." He ducked behind velvet drapes and observed Draven's reflection in a wall of gilded mirrors. The prince nursed his bourbon while trying to ignore the club owner's chatter. Raimond's ears easily tapped into their conversation.

"That doctor is the kindest guest you've ever brought here, Mr. Norman." Cleo wiped the bar clean and topped off his drink. "Does he plan to open a practice in town?"

"If everything goes according to his wishes, which I have misgivings about. . ." Draven flicked his hand in Raimond's direction. "He'll be employed by The Sisters of the Peace."

"The new hospital they're building on Gravier and Magazine?" Cleo clapped her hands. "I can't wait to tell my friends! So many of us older folks have no one—"

"Please, madam. It's still a secret." Draven pointed to the cigars. "Hernsheim Brothers?"

"Your favorite, La Belle Creole." Cleo plucked a cigar from the box and inhaled the aroma. "Best of luck in your search for a wife."

Draven let his forehead fall to the bar. "Don't you have customers to overcharge?"

Cleo made a zipping motion across her lips and danced away.

"That was quick." Draven perked up at the sound of Raimond's emergence from the back room. Instead of a smug and indulged companion, he watched Melody show off the bone medallion around her neck and explain the meaning of each symbol etched in its surface. "And unbelievable." Draven polished off his own drink and proceeded to drain Raimond's glass. He drummed his fingers on the bar until he had everyone's attention. "At least she's a young one. Shall we move along?"

Raimond dropped a generous tip in the piano player's jar on his way out.

Chapter 28

THE HALL OF VILLAINS

RAIMOND TRAILED THE prince through crowded streets, pausing at each bar's doorway to marvel at the amount of people celebrating in every available corner. He read the street signs as they walked. "Bienville?"

"Constructed the first levees." Draven shook his head. "Woefully inadequate mounds of dirt."

"And Iberville?"

"We're on Customhouse Street."

Raimond pointed up at a shiny sign.

"I wish they would stop changing street names. Iberville was a naval hero and explorer." Draven strode up to glass doors and allowed hotel doormen to sweep them open. "Died of yellow fever, or so they say."

Raimond shook a doorman's hand and grinned at the infusion of knowledge he gained. "This building is elegant. The total opposite of our last stop."

"It's quite the jewel, though not my favorite hotel." Draven walked directly toward a spinning red and white pole and sat down in an empty chair. "I have a standing appointment and a private barber—best in town. I suggest you have a shave as well. Lot's more people to meet before sunrise."

"Isn't tonight the—"

"Longest night of the year?" Draven winked and leaned back while a barber draped his neck in steaming towels. "We'll need every minute."

Within the hour both men passed through the back door of the hotel and into a residential alley.

"The shop on the corner belongs to a painter and metal sculptor." Draven undid a button on his shirt. "It's always sweltering in his studio, but the cloves—"

"I smell them from here." Raimond walked straight through the soaring French doors, inhaling the rich scent with deep breaths. "Heavenly."

Draven admired the jumble of art while Raimond negotiated a sale and filled his pockets with hand-rolled cigarettes. He paid for another carton to be picked up later.

"And who is this little beauty?" Raimond knelt and offered his hand to a grey dog.

"That's Faith," the artist answered. "She keeps me company when I burn the midnight oil."

"Pleased to meet you, Miss Faith." Raimond scratched her ears and she crawled into his arms. "Your work is beautiful, sir. Tell me about these birds."

"Faith doesn't warm up to everyone. You must be special." The artist shrugged and explained his process. "I don't care if people buy these paintings or not. I make them for myself. Some pelicans are so rare, I only see one pair a year."

"That's disheartening." Raimond spied Draven outside, sampling his cloves and blowing halos in the air. "Why do you think that is?"

"People encroaching on the wildlife, chasing them away." The artist nodded to the doorway. "Your companion is an impatient one. Best not keep him waiting any longer."

"Since I've just moved to town," Raimond dropped all the silver he had into the artist's hands, "I'd be honored if you considered me a patron."

With the packages securely tucked under a cluttered counter, Raimond joined Draven in the street and followed him past the chaos of a construction site. "Seems like an immense project."

"Maybe an enormous disaster. I've seen the plans. I fear it won't blend with the neighborhood." Draven pointed to a cupola on a building at the corner of Rues Chartres and St. Louis. "Know who that was built for?"

Raimond held his palms out. "You?"

"Definitely not my style. The intended resident was Napoleon Bonaparte. Tragically, he never arrived." Draven pointed his thumb down. "Might have been poison."

"Or maybe it was—" Raimond stopped at the corner and grabbed a twisted magnolia tree for support. "There's an awful vibe—I can't continue."

"No magic will ever cleanse this spot. Slaves were auctioned here, families brutally torn apart."

"I witnessed the atrocities of the Civil War in person." Raimond wobbled again.

"Maybe if you'd stop trying to absorb so much virtue, wickedness wouldn't be such a dagger to the heart."

Raimond grabbed his head and fell to his knees.

"All right, I've got you." Draven hauled him up and away from the hellish fog that began to clear within half a block. "What humans can do to each other is unfathomable. And they call vampires evil."

Raimond stopped to regain his composure. "Isn't this your favorite hotel? I see the gold dome."

"Truth be told, objectionable practices took place in the grand lobby of this establishment too, but I've had it blessed by every priestess and clergyman I could find. You should be able to walk through without the pain you felt on that damned corner."

"We aren't stopping here now?" Raimond crossed the street and peeked through curtained windows at more sparkling chandeliers. "My goodness."

"Later. Your record of lineage will be ready by sunrise." Draven held both hands up and for the first time all night, he waited for the

Royal Guard to close a supernatural barrier around them. The bustling corner of Rues Royale and St. Louis froze while they crossed and resumed seconds later, as if nothing happened. "Now, for your formal introduction to the leaders in this irreverent city."

"This is the place?" Raimond stepped back to admire arched second story galleries with cascading flowers that rivaled any he had seen during his tour. "With the underground room?"

"The hall of villains." Draven nodded to a senior guard. "Raimond, follow my lead."

Tall Ronald opened a beveled glass door draped with tiered lace curtains. "The location is swept and secure, boss."

Inside, another soldier presented Draven with the suit jacket he had shrugged off in the brick courtyard hours ago.

"Freshly pressed." Raimond slipped into his own coat. "Impeccable service."

Draven strode through a main dining room, set with square tables and snowy white linen. "No stopping, no talking. Everyone here is a potential enemy."

The descent below street level already blazed with enough torches to guide a blind man to the promised land. Their destination was a long room, painted emerald green and accented in sterling silver. The crowns of kings and queens along with ceremonial jewels lined each wall in sealed glass cases. The grandest of chandeliers lit the room with a kaleidoscope of vibrant reflection.

"Attention!" The senior guard's voice boomed from the doorway. "His Royal Highness, Prince Draven Norman."

A booming thud rattled crystal and silverware as every being in attendance dropped to one knee. Draven strode to the head of a lavishly set table and motioned for Raimond to follow. Surrounded by immaculate crystal and priceless wine, an inlaid fleur-de-lis shone in the center of the polished cypress.

"The second table?" Raimond whispered.

Draven nodded. "Whoever has the missing piece to complete the set, holds devastating power."

"All rise, Vampires of New Orleans." The prince lifted his eyes and the chamber plummeted into silence. "It is my royal pleasure to introduce the newest member of the Norman family. Duke Raimond Banitierre will assume control of our most hallowed city, and I expect every subject to show him the same respect you would my father, the king."

Raimond knelt and Draven repeated the ceremony with his jeweled dagger, this time in front of a room of witnesses.

The newly appointed duke stood to stare at a sea of blank faces, amidst a vibe that wasn't entirely friendly. When he spoke, his words resonated like the call to arms from a born commander. "I look forward to working with each of you to build an empire that's the envy of every royal family around the globe."

Coven leaders stepped forward, in order of power and pedigree, to greet Raimond. Draven offered a private word of wisdom or warning about each one as they departed.

The final man made even the brilliantly lit room shiver with chill.

"You've just met Cole Victoire." Draven faked a smile. "Above all, do not trust that snake. If he gives you reason to end him, seize the opportunity."

The ceremony concluded with a toast. Crystal goblets were filled with ancient blood. Draven raised his glass and every vampire in the room followed. "To Duke Banitierre and the immortal spirit of our majestic city!"

Chapter 29

Boneyard Eyes

WITH THE CEREMONY complete, Draven extricated himself from the underground room and signaled for a hot towel. He scoured his palms with an exaggerated sigh, shrugged out of his dinner jacket and donned a grey cloak. "Your coat is ready too, Raimond."

"Costume change?" Raimond slipped into the long black version.

"My after-midnight attire." Draven nodded to the guards. "Now, we can see that cathedral you've been lusting for since sunset...if you're ready."

"Its silhouette draws me like a magnet." The instant the doors opened, an invisible force plucked Raimond from the ruthless silence of the restaurant and thrust him into the street.

The portal to his past vanished into the mist as the present embraced him in a blanket of weighty incense and tropical fragrance. Beings crammed every inch of space. Ghosts, phantoms, demons and humans shook hands, shared drinks and danced in the lamplight as if united by a single spirit.

He struggled for words and turned back to Tall Ronald with a frown. "How does one define that sound?"

"Folks down here have their own descriptions. Hot. Low down." Ronald held up one finger at a time as bells chimed across the mismatched rooftops. "Glorious and ratty..."

Dueling clarinets blended with the joyful greeting of a violin and the somber reply of a cello. Around the corner, a jubilant trumpet traded breaths with the mournful push and pull of a lone saxophone. Beneath it all, the rhythmic pulse of tribal drums mimicked the heartbeat of a mystical lady.

"I've got it! Raimond tapped his ear. "Raggedy!"

"Hard to believe this is your first visit to the Crescent City, sir." Ronald swept his arm out to Rue Royale and grinned. "Fair warning, once you start dancing, you will never stop."

Raimond didn't feel his feet walking along the uneven cobblestones. Unconsciously, he veered into a dim alley and stopped short of the massive stone façade. "Can I touch this?"

Draven took a step back. "You may try."

Raimond caressed the church wall. The ground rumbled in waves and he recoiled, massaged his palm and laid it on the polished stone again.

A bartender bolted out of a dark doorway, rushing into the suddenly empty passage. "What the devil was that?" He crossed his arms and stared at Draven.

Draven pointed to Raimond and gave a half shrug. "Nice to see you too, Jeffrey."

"That's your newly appointed Duke?" Jeffrey pulled the bar towel off his shoulder and snapped it as he walked away. "I assumed you were aiming for stability, not more bedlam."

Draven dragged his feet, glancing back at Raimond twice before stepping into a corner bar. Behind the counter, Jeffrey filled a glass with green liquor and floated bitters. He dunked a sugar cube, placed it on a silver spoon and lit it with a match. After lowering the flaming cube into a glass and pouring ice water over the flames, the bartender served his masterpiece with a flourish.

Draven took a whiff of the Absinthe and stared into the street.

"What, you don't want it now?" Jeffrey huffed. "After all that work."

"I'm sure you've heard that the steel rails quivered?" Draven mumbled. "Nearly melted when the new duke crossed over?"

"That is no secret. To be fair, nothing is."

"It's never happened for me." Draven sipped the concoction and grimaced. "Not once, in all these years."

Raimond stumbled through the crooked door, gesturing at the church. "The first time I touched it, I saw things. Visions."

"I'm almost afraid to ask." Draven traded looks with Jeffrey. "Of what?"

Raimond scrubbed at his skin. "A nasty jumble of tattoos that sprung up my arms."

"Calm down before you draw blood." Draven grabbed his hands. "Like Faison's?"

"Yes, but different." Raimond pulled away. "I saw a blinding white room, raging fire and drooling tigers. I heard a full orchestra playing the waltz." He paused. "And then there was this woman."

Draven leaned in. "Do tell."

"A terrified young girl, really." Raimond sampled the Absinthe and pushed it away.

"Nobody likes this?" Jeffrey sniffed it and took a sip. "Tastes perfect."

"Go on, Raimond…" Draven glared at the bartender until he gave a flippant shrug. "Describe the girl."

"She had on a sapphire gown and a brilliant string of diamonds that wore her more than she wore them."

"And?" Jeffrey drummed his fingers on the bar.

"She was holding my dagger." Raimond glanced back at fog billowing from the cathedral garden and crumpled onto a bar stool, gasping. "The same blade that killed Faison."

Jeffrey forced a thin smile and poured Raimond straight bourbon. Both he and Draven watched the new duke drift to the door and collapse against the warped frame.

"So, Your Highness," Jeffrey whispered, "you must really dislike him."

"Quite the opposite," Draven answered. "He's kind and caring. The sort of fresh start this city needs."

"Sounds like a fatal flaw."

Draven raised his eyebrow.

"To be clear." Jeffrey jerked his head toward Raimond's back and held up his hands. "You put a kind and caring man—"

"A kind and caring doctor." Draven patted his chest. "With the heart of a rebel."

"Fine. Rebellious vampire, doctor, whatever." Jeffrey tossed cocktail olives over his shoulder. "In charge of a viper pit."

"Oh and the serpents were out in full force tonight." Draven grabbed an empty tumbler and motioned to the narrow door in a back corner. "I have your usual payment, but also another favor to ask."

Jeffrey refilled a few drinks on the house and joined Draven in a room small enough to be a closet. He accepted the usual pouch of coins and gulped a cup of fresh blood faster than he could taste it, grudgingly choked down a second and turned green.

"That should hold you for a while." After a minute, he held out a decorative coin stamped with the silver shield and ivy crest of the Norman empire. "As you've served me all these years, I now request that you to devote all your resources to the protection of House Banitierre."

Jeffrey rolled the coin in his palm and whistled. "You'll educate him on the finer details of our affairs and who to trust?"

"Yes, essentially nobody," Draven grunted. "Until he builds a family of his own, anyway. Kindly make sure he isn't poisoned by low-level thugs."

"That I can do." Jeffrey peeked out the door to make sure no one was eavesdropping. "Does it concern you that he's already seeing things? Crazy nonsense?"

"Show me someone who doesn't see things in this bizarre city," Draven shoved the old door open, "and I'll show you a liar."

Jeffrey lifted the empty bourbon glass off the bar. He stiffened when Raimond seized his wrist.

"Pleased to meet you, Mr. Jeffrey." Raimond released his grip. "I have exceptional hearing."

"Duly noted, Duke Banitierre."

Draven nudged Raimond's elbow. "We have one more important appointment to keep before sunrise."

Walking through the narrow alley next to the cathedral, Raimond stretched his fingers out to graze the stone again and changed his mind at the last minute. Each stained-glass window acknowledged him with simple grace notes from phantom bagpipes. He reached Rue Chartres and paced backwards across the flagstones, oblivious of pedestrians and carriage traffic that swerved to avoid him. His full attention was on spires that impaled the night sky. He finally turned around amidst a square of red buildings shielded by lace iron and gas lamps that twinkled in every window. He didn't stop walking until a towering bronze statue blocked his path.

"Raimond Banitierre, meet General Jackson." Draven motioned for security to tighten their perimeter. "We shouldn't linger out in the open."

Chasing the prince's quick steps, Raimond couldn't help but notice the fortune teller, a trio of musicians and two disheveled painters averting their eyes and granting them a wide berth.

An older woman flaunting painted skin marched across the grass with purpose. She intercepted the royal party before they reached the gate on Decatur Street. Security guards grabbed both her arms.

"Please, Your Highness." She sunk to her knees, craning her neck to keep Raimond in her sights. "May I have one moment of the new duke's time?"

"Let her speak." Draven impatiently motioned to his guards to set her free. "She's Roussel. Her family is loyal to us."

"Duke, my ancestors and I welcome you to our home." The woman held out her worn palms. "But I sense you're troubled. May I help?"

"No. I mean, thank you…yes. There is one thing." Raimond helped her stand. "The images that flooded my mind when I touched your beautiful cathedral—they were violent and disturbing."

"Visions such as those can't be eliminated completely. But I can cast them to another."

"Is that wise?" Draven asked. "Might they be warnings?"

"Possibly." The woman touched Raimond's cheek. "More often, snippets of memory and ancient curses search for an entity strong enough to harbor their magic. You, the man who rippled steel, are their perfect vessel."

"If I push that responsibility onto someone else." Raimond gazed at the sky. The fringes of a storm roiled over the jagged skyline. "Does it make me a coward?"

"Not at all. In fact, many with the gift to see would relish the drama. Gracious Lord—" The woman yanked her hand back and crept closer in one movement. "Gargoyles, angels and crosses…you have the boneyard eyes."

"I beg your pardon?" Draven stared at Raimond. "I see nothing."

"All I need is a lock of your hair and the visions will become the burden of the next eligible soul." She trembled. "Eventually."

Lightning vaulted between clouds and thunder echoed through the narrow streets.

"Holy hell!" Raimond grabbed the side of his head. His fingers sunk all the way to his skull. "Was that necessary?"

"Must be something in the water." On the tip of his jeweled dagger, Draven presented the painted lady with a clump of Raimond's hair and scalp, oozing black blood. "Everyone here is mad."

Chapter 30

CHARITY

IN AN UNLIT building on the corner of Gravier and Magazine Streets, Raimond followed Draven up six flights of stairs. The climb went from narrow to rough to under construction by the time they reached the top. "Isn't this a bit dusty and undignified for you, Your Highness?"

"Though I don't pretend to understand the reasons, you seem determined to remain a doctor."

"It's my calling."

"Very well, maybe I can use it to my advantage." Draven tore off old boards blocking the roof exit. "I'd love the newly appointed Mother Superior to stop nagging me for assistance."

"Did I meet her tonight?"

"Not yet." Draven nodded to a raven-haired woman leading a blind man through another open door. "Now's your chance."

"She's so…" Raimond whispered.

"Young? She's a force of nature." Draven shoved him ahead. "See for yourself."

"*Bonsoir*, I'm Commander, I mean, Dr. Banitierre." Raimond held out his hand and smiled at the pretty lady. "You're not dressed as a—"

"Nun?" She guided the elderly man to a bench and handed him his cornet before accepting Raimond's handshake. "I'm a bit unconventional."

Draven pointed at Raimond. "So is he."

"Mr. Norman has told me about you, Doctor."

"Call me Raimond, please." He rubbed his chin. "What has he revealed, exactly?"

She twisted the church's wedding ring on her finger and winked. *"Je m'appelle Charmaine."*

"I'm delighted to make your acquaintance, most honorable Charmaine." Raimond swept his coat out behind him and sunk to one knee. "What else do you know of my story?"

Charmaine caught her breath. "That you're a talented surgeon. We have quite a tremendous problem with injuries from criminal acts."

"I have the experience to handle that, and I can provide transcripts."

"No need. I already have a portfolio of recommendations for you, from an eclectic mix of creatures." She tipped her head. "Not all human."

Raimond gaped at Draven and then back at her. "He's right, I am a bit odd but…"

"This is New Orleans, Raimond. I'd be worried if you weren't," Charmaine said. "Since you sound serious about working in our hospital, I'll also warn you upfront, we have a large elderly population."

"They are my specialty." Raimond stood and pressed his palms together. "My forté."

She exhaled and smiled. "I'll expedite the hiring process."

"And I absolutely accept the position."

"Splendid." Draven stepped back and swept his hand out to the horizon. "Survey your new kingdom."

"That's a bit premature, don't you—" Raimond jumped as a flask was jammed into his hand. "Thank you, *madame*."

"Don't forget to share." She motioned to Draven. "He wants to make a toast, probably two."

"Reverend Mother." Draven bowed. "I welcome your input at any time."

"The city looks very different from this vantage point." Raimond's gaze traveled upriver and then back toward the Vieux Carré. Strains of music, laughter and the rhythm of countless heartbeats swirled on their way to heaven. "The chaos is mesmerizing."

"Appears harmless from up here." Draven chuckled. "But we all know better."

"I'd still like to see the mansions you described." Raimond grinned.

"Tomorrow night." Draven clapped his hands twice. "My private tour continues straight up St. Charles Avenue. An entirely unique playground."

Raimond zeroed in on the cathedral. "What is it about those three steeples? They're blacker than the blackest sky. Yet, they glow."

"The jewel of our skyline." Charmaine nodded her head. "Untapped power is hidden there."

The blind man behind them blew a long, crying note on his cornet.

"Booze, please!" Draven snapped his fingers at the flask and stepped onto the low wall overlooking the street. At the first slow hints of a tango, the prince wobbled.

"Mr. Norman?" Charmaine held out her arm to steady him.

Draven grasped her hand and jumped off the ledge with a flourish. He walked her backwards, alternating slow and quick steps.

Charmaine mirrored his moves. "You're a talented dancer."

"As are you, Reverend Mother." Draven pivoted and allowed the horn's flow to guide them to the roof's corners and back.

"Don't forget," Charmaine smiled and broke their embrace, "I've taken vows to the church."

"Of course. Though it does seem a shame." Draven uncapped the silver flask. "Would you ask why he chose to play that piece?"

The musician answered immediately, "You have the aura of a lonely man who loves to tango, Mr. Norman. And for the new gentleman…" The next notes were the unmistakable, three-quarter time of a gentle waltz.

Charmaine offered Raimond her hand. "Would you like to?"

"With pleasure." The melody's rise and fall under a star-laden sky drew her close enough for Raimond to feel her arms tremble and see her skin blush.

"Dear friends, must I remind you both of those inconvenient, holy vows?" Draven smirked and raised the flask before he sipped. "If I'm the chaperone, we're all doomed."

Charmaine sighed and stepped back. "I do hope we have the pleasure again." She swept tendrils of hair back and secured them in a loose knot. "Very soon."

"Don't let anyone break the harmony created on this roof tonight." The cornetist winked and blew a mix of triple beats with eclectic flow. "All souls crave love, and there's no better place to find it than Louisiana."

"Raimond, I know I've discouraged your interest in anyone who isn't young." Draven's expression drifted with the melody. "But if you insist on saving the older generation, make sure you take the best care of that musician. He brought back memories both sad and treasured." Draven ran a hand over his face. "But that's a discussion for another time."

New Orleans stretched out like a dreamscape around them. Masts of sailing ships were silhouetted against the moonlit river and candlelight twinkled through lace-iron balconies. In the distance, silver moss draped like fine silk from massive oaks. No matter how brilliant the glow of the city, darkness always devoured it like a ravenous predator chewing at the edges of civilization.

"To the macabre joy, preposterous hope and decadent celebration." Draven swallowed a mouthful of bourbon and saluted the moon. "To the only place where holy women, healers and horn players are true royalty."

"Where monsters and angels walk hand in hand." Charmaine grabbed the flask and took a healthy swig. "*Bienvenue*, Raimond. I welcome you and wish you all the wisdom of my ancient bloodline."

Draven intercepted the bourbon again. "Duke, prepare your wits and that dazzling smile. You'll need every weapon at your disposal in the eternally wicked revelry of this city."

"To my new home." Raimond finally held the flask in his hand. He brandished it to the skyline. "To New Orleans."

Epilogue
ENTER THE ANGELS
NEW ORLEANS, APRIL 1936

LONG AFTER DUSK, Raimond shoved heavy shutters away from the single window in a closet he called his office. The frame around the glass resisted being raised. He forced it and the pane fractured in the corner.

Again? Maintenance threatened to send me a bill the last time.

Raimond jammed the window up a few more inches until heavy river air flooded the tiny room.

How I've fallen in love with this city and her people. A society so unique…

His eyes traveled around the Mississippi's bend, where the outline of ships' smokestacks had replaced sailing masts.

Intrigued by back-room corruption. Entertained by duels in the park.

As if paying respect to the dismal block that used to be a grand opera house, only a few electric signs broke the spell of flickering gas lamps lining the French Quarter streets. Canal Street, however, was ablaze with modern illumination.

Cursed by violence and crime. Blessed by ritual and passion.

A relentless, rhythmic pulse mixed with snippets of harmony drifted on the breeze.

So many changes, yet the heartbeat remains the same and forever at the mercy of Mother Nature.

A gust of wind blew one file off his jumbled desk. An avalanche of documents followed.

This paperwork. Who has time to be a doctor anymore?

Raimond sighed, scooped up the pile and sorted it into two stacks—Sisters of the Peace or International Mission. He plunked into his chair with the mission batch in his hand. Each folder was stenciled with a single word: Charity.

"I need to see Dr. Banitierre. Move!" The office door flew open, slamming a coat rack into the wall hard enough to splinter plaster. A man barged in. "You can't stop me. I'm reporting that little bitch—"

"Dr. Winters—mind your tongue!" A nun stormed up behind him. "That young lady—"

"You nurses are all alike." Dr. Winters straightened his short white coat.

"Enough, Winters. Calm down." Raimond tossed his papers aside. "Reverend Mother, what is the trouble at this hour?"

"She's a liar."

"Winters," Raimond hissed. "Take a seat."

"But I was assault—"

Raimond stood and Dr. Winters dropped into a metal chair. "*S'il vous plait, Charmaine.*"

"That's her first name?" Dr. Winters snickered. "Thought they were all Marys."

Raimond forced himself to unclench his fists.

"Apparently, one of my newest nurses knocked this…" Charmaine gritted her teeth. "Resident on the floor."

"Twice. The nerve. The gall!" Dr. Winters held up his hands. "Sorry, sir."

"The young lady's file is on your desk." Charmaine pointed to the mess and shook her head. "The green one, on the bottom."

Out of the mission pile, Raimond dusted off a Charity binder.

"Give me a break," Dr. Winters mumbled. "Too many freeloaders. That's why this hospital is in such a state."

"Miss Sss…" Raimond ignored him and squinted hard at the first page. "My Gaelic pronunciation is dreadful—Miss Alden?"

Charmaine nodded. "From New York."

"Oh yes, St. Margaret's. I remember that application." Raimond's nod turned into a head-shake. "No, I haven't made the time to meet her yet."

"Who cares what her name is or what hole she crawled out of?" Dr. Winters slammed his fists on the chair. "What matters are the events of tonight."

"You're right." Charmaine crossed her arms with precision. "Let's talk about that disaster."

"I wrote the incident up right away, sir." Dr. Winters handed over a folded sheet of paper and sat back with a smug grin. "To make sure I didn't leave out any details."

Raimond read the first paragraph. "So, it seems you were knocked on your—" He flicked his eyes to Charmaine. "Knocked down by a girl. You needed notes for this?"

Dr. Winters adjusted his tie. "It was a criminal act."

Raimond finished the account, pausing a few times to glare at his resident. Finally, he placed the paper on his desk and tightened his jaw. "You were in Miss Marion's room. Why?"

"Pardon?" Dr. Winters swallowed hard. "You mean the old-as-dirt woman?"

"The patient." Raimond growled. "Marion d'Planchiette."

"I can't be expected to remember all the ridiculous southern names."

"Have you considered a career in pathology?" Raimond shot Charmaine a grim frown. "Because your bedside manner—"

"Raimond." She stared at his face and shook her head.

"Is barely appropriate—" Raimond cleared his desk in one violent sweep of his arm, "—for dead people!"

"Raimond!" Charmaine grabbed the rosary around her neck and crossed her heart.

"Yes, fine." Dr. Winters jumped back and tumbled over his chair. "Yes, I was in Marion Whoever's room. Practicing."

"Stabbing her in the neck with a huge needle." Charmaine inched toward him. "With a bloody drape over Marion's face. Suffocating her."

"Says who?" Dr. Winters jabbed his finger in the nun's face. "Your precious little nurse?"

"Did Marion consent?" Charmaine slapped his finger away.

Raimond held his hand up. "I want to hear his answer."

"Consent? Of course not. That woman has never uttered a word." Dr. Winters flicked his wrist. "This is a learning institution. She's a—"

"A what?" Raimond leaned on his desk. "Finish that statement."

"A vegetable."

Silence sucked the air out of the room.

"This conversation is over." Fire blazed under Raimond's skin. He fought to keep the black ribbons of blood hidden. *"C'est fini."*

"I'd like to be here when you interrogate her." Dr. Winters pulled a pen out of his pocket.

"Get out," Raimond growled.

"Where do I sign?"

Raimond caught the scent of roses and bleach from Charmaine's racing heart. "Fired."

"I'd recommend not being too hard on that simple girl." Winters clicked his pen twice. "Don't toss her in the street. She'll just end up in Emergency."

"She deserves a medal." Raimond loomed closer. "You're fired. Leave."

"With cuts and bruises, if not something worse." Dr. Winters laughed. "More work for everyone."

Raimond bolted across the desk and picked the man up by his throat. "Get the hell out!"

"Me?" Winters wheezed as Raimond shook him like a rag doll. "You're as insane as that nurse."

Charmaine yanked the door open and screamed into the hall. "Security!"

"Everything I've accomplished," Raimond dropped the resident on the floor and flashed his fangs, "you've undone in one night."

"Monster!" Winters scrambled back and brandished the coat rack like a sword. "Lord have mercy."

"Shut up, imbecile." Charmaine grabbed the coat rack and slammed it into the resident's forehead.

"Reverend Mother!" Raimond stumbled back.

"He hasn't ruined anything, but *you*—" She yanked her veil off. Long black waves fell around her shoulders. "—are about to."

Raimond spun away.

"Do whatever is necessary to alter his memory." Charmaine flattened her back against the door. Footsteps thundered in the hall. "Before the officers get here."

Raimond slapped Winters' face until he stirred. "Wake up, mindless weasel." Their eyes met and haze clouded the air. "Forget I attacked you. You're still fired. Run."

Dr. Winters sprung up and ploughed into hospital security. Charmaine unclipped the identification badge from his collar as he was dragged off.

"I am so sorry." Raimond sat on his desk and collapsed on his back. "Haven't lost my temper like that in, I don't know, years."

"Well nobody is perfect, but in your time here, you've done so much good for so many."

Raimond shook his head and blew out a long sigh. "A drop in the bucket of misery."

Charmaine propped her hands on her hips. "Show me your teeth."

Raimond displayed a fang-free, sheepish smile.

"Pretty close to perfect." She wrestled furniture back into position and scooped up papers. "Since you're medical director now, you need a bigger office."

"I know." Raimond jumped up and grabbed a pile of folders. He tucked some under his arm and jammed others on a crowded shelf. "Those charts are old."

"Then, for the love of God, sign them so the records department can file them." Charmaine planted current medical documents in the center of his desk. "What are you hiding?"

Raimond handed her the Charity pile. "I'm almost ready to announce our next mission trip."

"I know you placed the magazine advertisement." Charmaine flopped in the chair. "But after what happened, the last time we went to Nepal…those brutal animal attacks?"

"Security will be enhanced. I've already seen to it." Raimond walked around the desk. "There's so much suffering in the world. Doing nothing isn't an option."

"No. It is not." Charmaine shook her head. "But in the middle of all that carnage, I thought I'd never see Louisiana again."

"This new hospital is far away from those mountains. Much safer." Raimond squeezed her shoulder. "I promise, *madame*."

"Well, I hope you're right." Charmaine leaned over to pick up the last stray papers and braced herself against the floor. "Jesus, Mary and—"

Raimond flinched as she pulled the red-spined ledger from under his desk.

"What have I told you about no secret being safe in New Orleans? You were supposed to destroy this years ago!" She crushed her fist around the frayed edges. "I know Mr. Norman ordered you—if the wrong people find this thing, it's as good as a signed confession of heresy."

"I meant to, but the memories." Raimond jammed his hands in his pockets. "What if I forget—"

"You won't forget, my dear Raimond." Charmaine brushed her fingers against his cheek. "Every detail is locked away in your mind and your heart."

Raimond closed his eyes.

"You're a superb leader and remarkable mentor, but you get absorbed…carried away and a little complacent."

"It's a critical flaw. And I've paid for it dearly."

"I light a candle for your precious Emily every day."

Raimond dropped his chin and mouthed three silent words. *Praise the angels.*

"But if you're discovered," Charmaine grabbed his face with both hands, "if you're so much as accused, we're condemned. All of us."

"I need help. The last time I tried to burn it, down on the river bank, the fire fizzled out in seconds." Raimond pointed to the carved cover. "And now, these wings are blue."

"That means local magic has wormed its way in." She dumped a trash can and held the bin out until he dropped the book in. "Matches?"

"I've told you about Aveline, from Paris?" Raimond handed Charmaine a tin box from his desk drawer. "She cast the original spell."

"Hmm," Charmaine tugged on her earlobe and emptied the pockets of her habit. She tossed pens, bandage clips and syringes aside and kept digging until she held a red candle in her palm.

Raimond blinked hard, twice. "You cart all that rubbish around with you?"

"Always be prepared." Charmaine lit the wick, chanted words that made no sense and dropped the candle in the metal can. The book burst into flames.

"What about the smoke?" Raimond rushed to the window. "This barely opens."

"Do you see smoke?"

"No." Raimond peered into the trash bin. "No book either, just soot."

"Those," Charmaine pulled a foil bag from her pocket, poured the ashes in and sealed it with a silver clip, "are precious. Do you have a safe hiding spot?"

Raimond rolled open his desk drawer and slid back a hidden panel.

"Splendid." Charmaine placed the pouch in and stood back. "Right next to the big, scary blade."

"How terrifying can it be? It's a gift from my brother." Raimond picked up a pile of envelopes. "Please tell me we don't have to burn these too."

"Just simple family letters?" Charmaine traced the arcs and bends of script on yellowed parchment.

"*Oui, madame.*"

She eased the papers from his hands, tapped the edges square and gently replaced them in the drawer.

Raimond twirled an overloaded key ring around his finger. "Why are we saving the ashes of my diary, anyway?"

"Well, the journal isn't truly *gone*." Charmaine made quotation marks in the air with her fingers. "But it would take a specific witch, spell and the blood of your heir to reactivate it."

"That's all? Sounds safe to me." Raimond secured the panel and locked the drawer. "About your chant—those were no holy words I've ever heard."

"They're holy to somebody." Charmaine grabbed her veil. "Out of curiosity, what was Aveline's family name?"

"Roussel, I think."

Charmaine rolled down her sleeve and pointed to an embroidered R. "That's most likely why I was able to crack her spell."

"You too?" Raimond crouched down and slid in front of her. "Didn't you just lecture me about the danger of secrets?"

"Fair enough. The Roussels...their blood runs deep in New Orleans history."

"That's it? Are they all priests and nuns?"

"Heavens, no." Charmaine tossed her hands up. "Since you're planning a mission, I think it's time you met the new nurses."

Raimond grabbed the white coat off his chair and met her at the door. "You amaze me, Reverend Mother."

"You've certainly proved to me that all monsters are not created equal." Racket from the nurse's desk distracted her. "Oh my."

"Is that..." Raimond zeroed in on a group of nurses. "Miss Alden's first name—how do I pronounce the *ch*?"

"Sshh, like in champagne."

"Or Charmaine?" Raimond winked. "Got it."

"On the right, with the messy hair." Charmaine pointed down the hall. "Poor dear has been awake all night. Better hurry if you want to catch up."

"Yes, on my way." Raimond flipped his collar up and tousled his hair. "That young lady was brave enough to flip the world upside down, defending a patient. I need to meet Miss Sorcha Alden."

Acknowledgments

So many cast members, friends and fans have joined the *Monsters &* *Angels Society* in the past year...I'm overwhelmed with gratitude and appreciation.

First and foremost, I need to thank my husband Scott for surviving this crazy, novel-writing process again, for brainstorming gory details and the depths of vampire psyche in the middle of the night and for watching the entire final season of *The Originals* with me. I think I got him hooked on the show—he may never admit it.

Thank you, Adrian and Abby, for your everlasting Faith.

Gracious thanks to Jordan Rosenfeld, my editor; Dan Alatorre, my critique partner; Courtney McDermott, my proofreader, Eight Little Pages, my cover designers; Lynn Cozza, Crystal Lukacs, Victoria Clapton, Allison Maruska, Maggie Johnson, Heather Kindt, Racquel Kechagias, and Lauren Stroh, my beta-readers—each and every one offered the perfect words of encouragement when I needed them most. They also endured my French.

Merci beaucoup!

THE WAY MAY SOAR AND BEND,
THE FATED PLUNGE SHEER AND MEAN,
BUT IN THE GLORIOUS END,
ALL ROADS LEAD TO NEW ORLEANS...

About the Author

Anne Marie has been an equestrienne, chorale singer, EMT and baseball fan. Roaming the back roads of New Jersey with her family, she found great respect for antiques, historical locations and the stories they hold. Her current list of favorite pastimes includes coffee, bourbon and Les Misérables—which requires more bourbon. She has been known to attend sporting events just for the flyover. The boat she and her husband christened Glory Days, is her escape from the chaos of everyday life.

The inspiration for *Raimond* and *Monsters & Angels* is Anne Marie's fascination with vampires, castles and her passion for everything New Orleans. When she isn't writing, she can be found working nights with the critical care team in a busy trauma center.